TALES OF SE

Leo Tolstoy
Count Leo Nikolayevich Tolstoy was born in 1828 at Yasnaya Polyana in the Tula province of Russia, and educated privately. He fought in the Crimean war and after the defence of Sebastopol wrote *The Sebastopol Stories*, which established his reputation.

After a period in St Petersburg and abroad, where he studied educational methods for use in his school for peasant children in Yasnaya, he married Sofya Andreyevna Behrs in 1862. The next fifteen years was a period of great happiness; they had thirteen children and Tolstoy managed his vast estates in the Volga steppe, continued his educational projects, cared for his serfs and wrote *War and Peace* (1865-8) and *Anna Karenina* (1874-6).

His teaching earned him numerous followers in Russia and abroad, but also much opposition and in 1901 he was excommunicated by the Russian holy synod. He died in 1910 in the course of a dramatic flight from home, at the small railway station of Astapovo.

Richard Godwin is an arts journalist and columnist on the London *Evening Standard*. He studied French and Russian at New College, Oxford, and lives in London.

Tales of Sexual Desire

Tales of Sexual Desire
The Devil, The Kreutzer Sonata, Father Sergius

———————————

Leo Tolstoy

FOREWORD BY RICHARD GODWIN

CAPUCHIN CLASSICS

CAPUCHIN CLASSICS
LONDON

Tales of Sexual Desire

The Devil first published 1889
The Kreutzer Sonata first published 1889
Father Sergius first published 1898

This edition published by Capuchin Classics 2009

© Capuchin Classics 2009
2 4 6 8 0 9 7 5 3 1

Capuchin Classics
128 Kensington Church Street, London W8 4BH
Telephone: +44 (0)20 7221 7166
Fax: +44 (0)20 7792 9288
E-mail: info@capuchin-classics.co.uk
www.capuchin-classics.co.uk

Châtelaine of Capuchin Classics: Emma Howard
Translation editor: Anthony Guise

ISBN: 978-0-9555196-8-0

All rights reserved. No part of this publication
may be reproduced, stored in a retrieval system, or
transmitted in any form or by any means,
electronic, mechanical, photocopying, recording,
or otherwise, without the prior permission of the
copyright owner

Contents

Foreword 9

The Devil 15

The Kreutzer Sonata 69

Father Sergius 157

Foreword

Driven by irresistible sexual torment to its final, glorious act of penetration, Leo Tolstoy's *The Kreutzer Sonata* is among the most disquieting works of world literature. 'When reading it one can hardly refrain from exclaiming "That is the truth!" or "This is absurd!"' wrote Anton Chekhov amid the furore that followed the story's publication in 1889, provoked by Tolstoy's assault on the institution of marriage, plea for abstinence and gleefully murderous narrative. Even the American president Theodore Roosevelt was inspired to call the author a 'sexual moral pervert'.

Engaging with it now is scarcely less bracing, an affront to one's casual twenty-first century convictions. One modern critic has labelled it 'the ugliest, maddest thing ever written about sex and marriage by any major figure'. Others have accused Tolstoy of misogyny, misanthropy, even repressed homosexuality. Here, it is fair to say, the conflict between the spiritual, sensual and social that powers Tolstoy's writing reaches its darkest, bloodiest apotheosis.

For Tolstoy (1828-1910), the novella was the product of two years of profound unhappiness and religious conflict that led to his temporary abandonment of fiction in the mid-1880s. The origins of the plot lie in a fragment dating from the early 1860s entitled *The Wife-Murderer*, while the narrative structure and the central figure of Pozdnyshev were prompted by a chance meeting with a cuckold in a railway carriage. A performance in early 1888 of Beethoven's violin sonata gave the tale its tempo and title, yet the true thrust of the piece is rooted in Tolstoy's agonised sexual relations with his wife Sofia Behrs. The younger Tolstoy's romantic desire for a pure marriage that would put an end to his self-confessed perversions (reflected in Eugene in *The Devil*) had been eroded through thirty years of libidinal turmoil and mundane bickering. Now delivering his thirteenth child and devoting herself to preserving her husband's literary legacy, Sofia had come to inspire disgust in him, which frequently took violent form. *The Kreutzer Sonata* is, in large part, confession.

The exact dates of the composition of the final draft are unknown, though the awkward structure suggests much of it was completed quickly, powered by the force of dawning revelation. The narrative voice (Tolstoy at his most Dostoevskian) is itself unstable. The curious narrator who indulges Pozdnyshev's railway carriage monologue is a coy cipher; when Pozdnyshev takes flight (fuelled by his mysterious tea), we hear Tolstoy's voice wobbling through. Many of Pozdnyshev's revelations of married life are lifted directly from the author's own, while the convictions expressed, however crazy they appear, are fully felt, even if Tolstoy claimed chastity was an ideal rather than an absolute. 'The substance of what I was writing was just as new to me then as it is now to those who are reading it,' he wrote in a letter of 1890; 'at first I was stricken with horror and did not want to accept it; subsequently, however, I grew convinced of its truth, saw the error of my ways and rejoiced at the joyful transformation that awaited me and others.'

That the censors of Tsar Alexander III would seek the novella banned was a given; that their actions would only increase its *succès de scandale* more so, as readers eagerly distributed illegal lithographs and handwritten copies of the original manuscript. Sofia pulled a deft piece of literary sleight-of-hand for it to be published above ground, obeying the Tsar's decree that it could appear only as part of a 'Complete Works' so as to be priced out of the financial reach of the masses, while ensuring that those 'Complete Works' were made available volume by volume. Not surprisingly, sales of the slim, affordable thirteenth tome containing *The Kreutzer Sonata* far outstripped the others. Her troubles must be seen as her attempt to come to terms with a story which must have been humiliating in the extreme; as the devoted secretary of his legacy, she sought to legitimise her own unhappy tale, passing it off as art.

At root, Pozdnyshev's tract is a reversal of the famous opening to *Anna Karenina* – that all unhappy families are unhappy each in their own way. No longer: 'Everyone thinks his own miserable marriage is unique,' says Pozdnyshev, but 'ninety-nine per cent of all married couples live in the same hell I lived in, and this cannot be otherwise.'

The cause of this unhappiness is sex, which must provoke jealousy and hatred in both husband and wife for 'their co-operation in defiling a human being'. Even in the relatively civilised parts of nineteenth-century Russia, society resembles a kind of licensed brothel, where young girls of good family are whored by their parents to rich young men turned bestial by their desire.

Tolstoy found his response to the eponymous Beethoven sonata mirrored his attitude to sex: immense personal agitation followed by extreme self-revulsion and generalised indignation that such vices should be so widely indulged and exalted. 'How can one allow anyone who pleases to hypnotize another, or many others, and do what he likes with them?' thunders Pozdynshev. 'An awakening of energy and feeling unsuited both to the time and the place, to which no outlet is given, cannot act but harmfully.' (For impact, it is the Perlman/Ashkenazy recording on Decca, with its mix of passionate abandon and burlesque mockery, that chimes perfectly with the affair of Pozdnyshev's wife and Trukhachevsky, and illuminates the story vividly).

Tolstoy's shaky science is one of the aspects that caused Chekhov to cry absurdity. 'His remarks about syphilis, Foundling Hospitals, women's aversion to contraception, etc., are not merely open to dispute, but frankly reveal an ignorant man who during his long life has not taken the trouble to read a few books by specialists,' complained the doctor. Today, pathology and psychology have advanced to such a degree we many claims out of hand; certainly no one admires auto-castration as a remedy for widespread sexual frustration, as Tolstoy once did, citing the example of the American Shakers.

Given its excesses, the tale is thus frequently sidelined as a work notable principally for its place in Tolstoy's biography, and its significance in ushering in his final phase of writing (which led, too, to *The Devil* and *Father Sergius*). Yet *The Kreutzer Sonata* deserves to be taken seriously in and of itself – and not dismissed as the work of a man who, in today's climate of defensive permissiveness, would be instructed to 'lighten up'.

Simply, it stands at the beginning of a canon of modern literature that takes the insatiability of lust as its overriding theme – from DH Lawrence and James Joyce through to Philip Roth, John Updike and Michel Houellebecq, whose zeitgeist-capturing 1998 novel *Atomised* bears extremely close comparison. *The Kreutzer Sonata's* central idea must be even more urgent in today's hedonistic society, when sex, through advertising which must stimulate desire where there was none before, actively drives our global economy, and promiscuity is cited as the reason for the most dramatic attacks on Western culture. In the late nineteenth century, Tolstoy's hyper-sensitivity to sex led him to see it in places where few others could; in doing so, he could be astonishingly prescient. Take his description of woman subjugated sexually, seeking power through spending: 'Go round the shops in any big town! Look whether in any of these shops there is anything for the use of men. All the luxuries of life are demanded by and maintained by women! Millions of people, generations of slaves, perish in factories merely to satisfy women's caprices.'

Even if we disagree with the prescriptions, we can admire the perception, and even at his most melodramatic, Tolstoy's here is still masterful. Take Pozdnyshev's obsession with Trukhachevsky's 'specially developed posterior'; or the all-too-believable irritation Pozdnyshev's wife displays as she is discovered. Even that description of music as 'an awakening of energy and feeling unsuited both to the time and the place', in condemning captures its power. 'If the earth itself could write,' Isaak Babel said, 'it would write like Tolstoy.'

We must make ourselves eunuchs and let ourselves die out is Tolstoy's response to all this sin, quoting Matthew's gospel. To those who find this unacceptable, Tolstoy fires back: 'In defending our indulgence in sexual intercourse are we really concerned with the extinction of the species? What we are really concerned with is our own pleasure.' Harsh – but fair? Brace yourself.

Richard Godwin
London, September 2008

The Devil
[1889]*

*Tolstoy revised some of his stories several times. 'The Devil' (first published 1889) appears here with its revised 1909 ending.

But I say unto you, that every one that looketh on a woman to lust after her hath committed adultery with her already in his heart.

And if thy right eye offend thee, pluck it out, and cast it from thee: for it is profitable for thee that one of thy members should perish, and not thy whole body be cast into hell.

And if thy right hand causeth thee to stumble, cut it off, and cast it from thee: for it is profitable for thee that one of thy members should perish, and not thy whole body be cast into hell. Matthew 5: 28-30

I

A brilliant career lay before Eugène Irtenev. He had everything necessary to attain it: an admirable education at home, high honours when he graduated in law at Petersburg University, and connections in the highest society through his recently deceased father; he had also already begun service in one of the Ministries under the protection of the Minister. Moreover he had a fortune; even a large one, though insecure. His father had lived abroad and in Petersburg, allowing his sons, Eugène and Andrew (who was older than Eugène and in the Horse Guards), six thousand roubles a year each, while he himself and his wife spent a great deal. He used to visit his estate only for a couple of months in summer and did not concern himself with its direction, entrusting it all to an unscrupulous manager who also failed to attend to it, but in whom he had complete confidence.

After the father's death, when the brothers began to divide the property, so many debts were discovered that their lawyer even advised them to disown the inheritance and retain only an estate left them by their grandmother, which was valued at a hundred thousand roubles. But a neighbouring landed proprietor who had done business with old Irtenev, that is to say, who had promissory notes from him and had come to Petersburg on that account, said that in spite of the debts they could straighten out affairs so as to retain a large fortune (it would only be necessary to sell the forest and some outlying land, retaining the rich Semenov estate with four thousand *desyatins* of black earth, the sugar factory, and two hundred *desyatins* of water-meadows) if one devoted oneself to the management of the estate, settled there, and farmed it wisely and economically.

And so, having visited the estate in spring (his father had died in Lent), Eugène looked into everything, resolved to retire from the Civil Service, settle in the country with his mother, and undertake the management with the object of preserving the main estate. He arranged with his brother, with whom he was very friendly, that he would pay him either four thousand roubles a year, or a lump sum of eighty thousand, for which Andrew would hand over to him his share of the inheritance.

So he arranged matters and, having settled down with his mother in the big house, began managing the estate eagerly, yet cautiously.

It is generally supposed that 'conservatives' are usually old people, and that those in favour of change are the young. That is not quite correct. Usually 'conservatives' are young people: those who want to live but who do not think about how to live, and have not time to think, and therefore take as a model for themselves a way of life that they have seen.

Thus it was with Eugène. Having settled in the village, his aim and ideal was to restore the form of life that had existed, not in his father's time—his father had been a bad manager—but in his grandfather's. And now he tried to resurrect the general spirit of his grandfather's life—in the house, the garden, and in the estate management—of course with changes suited to the times—everything on a large scale—good order, method, and everybody satisfied. But to do this entailed much work. It was necessary to meet the demands of the creditors and the banks, and for that purpose to sell some land and arrange renewals of credit. It was also necessary to get money to carry on (partly by farming out land, and partly by hiring labour) the immense operations on the Semenov estate, with its four hundred *desyatins* of ploughland and its sugar factory, and to deal with the garden so that it should not seem to be neglected or in decay.

There was much work to do, but Eugène had plenty of strength—physical and mental. He was twenty-six, of medium height, strongly built, with muscles developed by gymnastics. He was full-blooded and his whole neck was very red, his teeth and lips were bright, and his hair soft and curly though not thick. His only physical defect was short-sightedness, which he had himself compounded by using spectacles, so that he could not now do without a pince-nez, which had already formed a line on the bridge of his nose.

Such he was physically. For his spiritual portrait it might be said that the better people knew him the better they liked him. His mother had always loved him more than anyone else, and now after her husband's death she concentrated on him not only her whole affection but her whole life. Nor was it only his mother who so loved him. All his comrades at the high school and the university not merely liked him very much, but respected him. He had this effect on all who met him. It was impossible not to believe what he said, impossible to suspect any deception or falseness in one who had such an open, honest face and in particular such eyes.

In general his personality helped him much in his affairs. A creditor who would have refused another trusted him. The clerk, the village elder, or a peasant, who would have played a dirty trick and cheated someone else, forgot to deceive under the pleasant impression of intercourse with this kindly, agreeable, and above all straightforward man.

It was the end of May. Eugène had somehow managed in town to get the vacant land freed from the mortgage, so as to sell it to a merchant, and had borrowed money from that same merchant to replenish his stock, that is to say, to procure horses, bulls, and carts, and in particular to begin to build a necessary farm-house. The matter had been arranged. The timber was being carted, the carpenters were already at work, and manure for the estate was being brought on eighty carts, yet everything still hung by a thread.

II

Amid these cares something came about which though unimportant tormented Eugène at the time. As a young man he had lived as all healthy young men live, that is, he had had relations with women of various kinds. He was not a libertine but neither, as he himself said, was he a monk. He only turned to this, however, in so far as was necessary for physical health and to have his mind free, as he used to say. This had begun when he was sixteen and had gone on satisfactorily—in the sense that he had never given himself up to debauchery, never once been infatuated, and had never contracted a disease. At first he had had a seamstress in Petersburg, then she got spoilt and he made other arrangements, and that side of his affairs was so well secured that it did not trouble him.

But now he was living in the country for the second month and did not at all know what he was to do. Compulsory self-restraint was beginning to have a bad effect on him.

Must he really go to town for that purpose? And where to? How? That was the only thing that disturbed him; but as he was convinced that the thing was necessary and that he needed it, it really became a necessity, and he felt that he was not free and that his eyes involuntarily followed every young woman.

He did not approve of having relations with a married woman or a wench in his own village. He knew by report that both his father and grandfather had been quite different in this matter from other landowners of that time. At home they had never had any entanglements with peasant-women, and he had decided that he would not do so either; but afterwards, feeling himself ever more and more under compulsion and imagining with alarm what might happen to him in the neighbouring country town, and reflecting on the fact that the days of serfdom were now over, he decided that it might be done on the spot. Only it must be done so that no one should know of it, and not for the sake of debauchery but merely for health's sake—as he said to himself. When he had decided this he became still more restless. When talking to the village elder, the peasants, or the carpenters, he involuntarily brought the conversation round to women, and when it turned to women he kept it on that theme. He noticed the women more and more.

III

To settle the matter in his own mind was one thing but to carry it out was another. To approach a woman himself was impossible. Which one? Where? It must be done through someone else, but to whom should he speak about it?

He happened to go into a watchman's hut in the forest to get a drink of water. The watchman had been his father's huntsman, and Eugène Ivanich chatted with him, and the man began telling some strange tales of hunting sprees. It occurred to Eugène Ivanich that it would be convenient to arrange matters in this hut, or in the wood, only he did not know how to manage it and whether old Daniel would undertake the arrangement. 'Perhaps he will be horrified at such a proposal and I shall have disgraced myself, but perhaps he will agree to it quite simply.' So he thought while listening to Daniel's stories. Daniel was telling how once when they had been stopping at the hut of the sexton's wife in an outlying field, he had brought a woman for Fedor Zakharich Pryanishnikov.

'It will be all right,' thought Eugène.

'Your father, may the kingdom of heaven be his, did not go in for nonsense of that kind.'

'It won't do,' thought Eugène. But to test the matter he said: 'How was it you were involved in such bad things?'

'But what was there bad in it? She was glad, and Fedor Zakharich was satisfied, very satisfied. I got a rouble. Why, what was he to do? He too is a lively limb apparently, and drinks wine.'

'Yes I may speak,' thought Eugène, and at once proceeded to do so.

'And do you know, Daniel, I don't know how to endure it,'— he felt himself going scarlet.

Daniel smiled.

'I am not a monk—I have been accustomed to it.' He felt that what he was saying was stupid, but was glad to see that Daniel approved.

'Why of course, you should have told me long ago. It can all be arranged,' said he: 'only tell me which one you want.'

'Oh, it is really all the same to me. Of course not an ugly one, and she must be healthy.'

'I understand!' said Daniel briefly. He reflected.

'Ah! There is a tasty morsel,' he began. Again Eugène went red. 'A tasty morsel. See here, she was married last autumn.' Daniel whispered,— 'and he hasn't been able to do anything. Think what that is worth to one who wants it!'

Eugène even frowned with shame.

'No, no,' he said. 'I don't want that at all. I want, on the contrary (what could the contrary be?), on the contrary I only want that she should be healthy and that there should be as little fuss as possible—a woman whose husband is away in the army or something of that kind.'

'I know. It's Stepanida I must bring you. Her husband is away in town, just the same as a soldier. And she is a fine woman, and clean. You will be satisfied. As it is I was saying to her the other day—you should go, but she . . .'

'Well then, when is it to be?'

'Tomorrow if you like. I shall be going to get some tobacco and I'll call in, and at the dinner-hour come here, or to the bath-house behind the kitchen garden. There'll be nobody about. Besides after dinner everybody takes a nap.'

'All right then.'

A terrible excitement seized Eugène as he rode home. 'What will happen? What is a peasant woman like? Suppose it turns out that she is hideous, horrible? No, she is handsome,' he told himself, remembering some he had been noticing. 'But what shall I say? What shall I do?'

He was not himself all that day. Next day at noon he went to the forester's hut. Daniel stood at the door and silently and significantly nodded towards the wood. The blood rushed to Eugène's heart, he was conscious of it and went to the kitchen garden. No one was there. He went to the bathhouse—there was no one about, he looked in, came out, and suddenly heard the crackling of a breaking twig. He looked round—and she was standing in the thicket beyond the little ravine. He hurried there across the ravine. There were nettles in it which he had not noticed. They stung him and, losing the pince-nez from his nose, he ran up the slope on the farther side. She stood there, in a white embroidered apron, a red-brown skirt, and a bright red kerchief, barefoot, fresh, firm, and handsome, and smiling shyly.

'There is a path leading round—you should have gone round,' she said. 'I came long ago, ever so long.'

He went up to her and, looking her over, touched her.

A quarter of an hour later they separated; he found his pince-nez, called in to see Daniel, and in reply to his question: 'Are you satisfied, master?' gave him a rouble and went home.

He was satisfied. Only at first had he felt ashamed, then it had passed off. And everything had gone well. The best thing was that he now felt at ease, tranquil and vigorous. As for her, he had not even seen her thoroughly. He remembered that she was clean, fresh, not bad-looking, and simple, without any pretence. 'Whose wife is she?' said he to himself. 'Pechnikov's,' Daniel said. What Pechnikov is that? There are two households of that name. Probably she is old Michael's daughter-in-law. Yes, that must be it. His son does live in Moscow. I'll ask Daniel about it some time.'

From then onward that previously important drawback to country life—enforced self-restraint was eliminated. Eugène's freedom of mind was no longer disturbed and he was able to attend freely to his affairs.

And the matter Eugène had undertaken was far from easy: before he had time to stop up one hole a new one would unexpectedly show itself, and it sometimes seemed to him that he would not be able to go through with it and that it would end in his having to sell the estate after all, which would mean that all his efforts would be wasted and that the had failed to accomplish what he had undertaken. That prospect disturbed him most of all.

All this time more and more debts of his father's unexpectedly came to light. It was evident that towards the end of his life he had borrowed right and left. At the time of the settlement in May, Eugène had thought he at last knew everything, but in the middle of the summer he suddenly received a letter from which it appeared that there was still a debt of twelve thousand roubles to the widow Esipova. There was no promissory note, but only an ordinary receipt which his lawyer told him could be disputed. But it did not enter Eugène's head to refuse to pay a debt of his father's merely because the document could be challenged. He only wanted to know for certain whether there had been such a debt.

'Mamma! Who is Valeriya Vladimirovna Esipova?' he asked his mother when they met as usual for dinner.

'Esipova? She was brought up by your grandfather. Why?'

Eugène told his mother about the letter.

'I wonder she is not ashamed to ask for it. Your father gave her so much!'

'But do we owe her this?'

'Well now, how shall I put it? It is not a debt. Papa, out of his unbounded kindness...'

'Yes, but did Papa consider it a debt?'

'I cannot say. I don't know. I only know it is hard enough for you without that.'

Eugène saw that Mary Pavlovna did not know what to say, and was as it were sounding him out.

'I see from what you say that it must be paid,' said he. 'I will go to see her tomorrow and have a chat, and see if it can't be deferred.'

'Ah, how sorry I am for you, but you know that will be best. Tell her she must wait,' said Mary Pavlovna, evidently reassured and proud of her son's decision.

Eugène's position was particularly hard because his mother, who was living with him, did not at all grasp his position. She had been so accustomed all her life long to live extravagantly that she could not even imagine to herself the position her son was in, that is to say, that today or tomorrow matters might shape themselves so that they would have nothing left and he would have to sell everything and live and support his mother on what salary he could earn, which at the very most would be two thousand roubles. She did not understand that they could only save themselves from that position by cutting down expense in everything, and so she could not understand why Eugène was so careful about trifles, in expenditure on gardeners, coachmen, servants—even on food. Also, like most widows, she nourished feelings of devotion to the memory of her departed spouse quite different from those she had felt for him while he was alive, and she did not admit the thought that anything the departed had done or arranged could be wrong or could be altered.

Eugène by great efforts managed to keep up the garden and the conservatory with two gardeners, and the stables with two coachmen. And Mary Pavlovna naively thought that she was sacrificing herself for her son and doing all a mother could do, by not complaining of the food which the old chef prepared, of the fact that the paths in the park were not all swept clean, and that instead of footmen they had only a boy.

So, too, concerning this new debt, in which Eugène saw an almost crushing blow to all his undertakings, Mary Pavlovna only saw an incident displaying Eugène's noble nature. Moreover she did not feel much anxiety about Eugène's position, because she was confident that he would make a brilliant marriage which would put everything right. And he *could* make a very brilliant marriage: she knew a dozen families who would be glad to give their daughters to him. She wished to arrange the matter as soon as possible.

IV

Eugène himself dreamt of marriage, but not in the same way as his mother. The idea of using marriage as a means of putting his affairs in order was repulsive to him. He wished to marry honourably, for love. He observed the girls whom he met and those he knew, and compared himself with them, but no decision had yet been taken. Meanwhile, contrary to his expectations, his relations with Stepanida continued, and even acquired the character of a settled affair. Eugène was so far from debauchery, it was so hard for him secretly to do this thing which he felt to be bad, that he could not arrange these meetings himself and even after the first one hoped not to see Stepanida again; but it turned out that after some time the same restlessness (due he believed to that familiar cause) again overcame him. And his restlessness this time was no longer impersonal, but brought to mind just those same bright, black eyes, and that deep voice saying, 'ever so long', that same scent of something fresh and strong, and that same full breast lifting the bib of her apron, and all this in that hazel and maple thicket, bathed in bright sunlight.

Though he felt ashamed he again approached Daniel. And again a rendezvous was fixed for midday in the wood. This time Eugène looked her over more carefully and everything about her seemed attractive. He tried talking to her and asked about her husband. He really was Michael's son and lived as a coachman in Moscow.

'Well, then, how is it that you . . .' Eugène wanted to ask how it was she was untrue to him.

'What about "how is it"?' asked she. Evidently she was clever and quick-witted.

'Well, how is it you come to me?'

'There now,' said she merrily. 'I bet he goes on the spree there. Why shouldn't I?'

Evidently she was putting on an air of sauciness and assurance, and this seemed charming to Eugène. But all the same he did not himself fix a rendezvous with her. Even when she proposed that they should meet without the aid of Daniel, to whom she seemed not very well disposed, he did not consent. He hoped that this meeting would be the last. He liked her. He thought such intercourse was necessary for him and that there was nothing bad about it, but in the depth of his soul there was a stricter judge who did not approve of it and hoped that this would be the last time, or if he did not hope that, at any rate did not wish to participate in arrangements to repeat it another time.

So the whole summer passed, during which they met a dozen times and always with Daniel's help. It happened once that she could not be there because her husband had come home, and Daniel proposed another woman, but Eugène declined with disgust. Then the husband went away and the meetings continued as before, at first through Daniel, but afterwards he simply fixed the time and she came with another woman, Prokhorova—as it would not do for a peasant-woman to go about alone.

Once at the very time fixed for the rendezvous a family came to call on Mary Pavlovna, with the very girl she wished Eugène to marry, and it was impossible for Eugène to get away. As soon as he could do so, he went out as though to the threshing-floor, and round by the path to their meeting-place in the wood. She was not there, but at the accustomed spot everything within reach had been broken—the black alder, the hazel-twigs, and even a young maple the thickness of a stake. She had waited, had become excited and angry, and had skittishly left him a remembrance. He waited and waited, and then went to Daniel to ask him to call her for tomorrow. She came and was just as usual.

So the summer passed. The meetings were always arranged in the wood, and only once, when it grew towards autumn, in the shed that stood in her backyard.

It did not enter Eugène's head that these relations of his had any importance for him. He did not even think about her. He gave her money and nothing more. At first he did not know and did not think that the affair was known and that she was envied throughout the village, or that her relations took money from her and encouraged her, and that her conception of any sin in the matter had been quite obliterated by the influence of the money and her family's approval. It seemed to her that if people envied her, then what she was doing was good.

'It is simply necessary for my health,' thought Eugène. 'I grant it is not right, and though no one says anything, everybody, or many people, know of it. The woman who comes with her knows. And once *she* knows she is sure to have told others. But what's to be done? I am acting badly,' thought Eugène, 'but what's one to do? Anyhow it's not for long.'

What chiefly disturbed Eugène was the thought of the husband. At first for some reason it seemed to him that the husband must be a poor sort, and this as it were partly justified his conduct. But he saw the husband and was struck by his appearance: he was a fine fellow and smartly dressed, in no way a worse man than himself, but surely better. At their next meeting he told her he had seen her husband and had been surprised to see that he was such a fine fellow.

'There's not another man like him in the village,' said she proudly.

This surprised Eugène, and the thought of the husband tormented him still more after that. He happened to be at Daniel's one day and Daniel, having begun chatting, said to him quite openly: 'And Michael asked me the other day: "Is it true that the master is living with my wife?" I said I did not know. "Anyway," I said, "better with the master than with a peasant."'

'Well, and what did he say?'

'He said: "Wait a bit. I'll get to know and I'll give it her all the same."'

'Yes, if the husband returned to live here I would give her up,' thought Eugène.

But the husband lived in town and for the present their intercourse continued.

'When necessary I will break it off, and there will be nothing left of it,' he thought.

And this seemed to him certain, especially as during the whole summer many different things occupied him very fully: the erection of the new farmhouse, and the harvest, and above all meeting the debts and selling the wasteland. All these were affairs that completely absorbed him and on which he spent his thoughts when he lay down and when he got up. All that was real life. His intercourse—he did not even call it connection— with Stepanida he paid no attention to. It is true that when the wish to see her arose it came with such strength that he could think of nothing else. But this did not last long. A meeting was arranged, and he again forgot her for a week or even for a month.

In autumn Eugène often rode to town, and there became friendly with the Annenskis. They had a daughter who had just finished the Institute. And then, to Mary Pavlovna's great grief, it happened that Eugène 'cheapened himself', as she expressed it, by falling in love with Liza Annenskaya and proposing to her.

From that time his relations with Stepanida ceased.

V

It is impossible to explain why Eugène chose Liza Annenskaya, as it is always impossible to explain why a man chooses this and not that woman. There were many reasons—positive and negative. One reason was that she was not a very rich heiress such as his mother sought for him, another that she was naive and to be pitied in her relations with her mother, another that she was not a beauty who attracted general attention to herself, and yet she was not bad looking. But the chief reason was that his acquaintance with her began at the time when he was ripe for marriage. He fell in love because he knew that he would marry.

Liza Annenskaya was at first merely pleasing to Eugène, but when he decided to make her his wife his feelings for her became much stronger. He felt that he was in love.

Liza was tall, slender, and long. Everything about her was long; her face, and her nose (not prominently but downwards), and her fingers, and her feet. The colour of her face was very delicate, creamy white and delicately pink; she had long, soft, and curly, light-brown hair, and beautiful eyes, clear, mild, and confiding. Those eyes especially struck Eugène, and when he thought of Liza he always saw those clear, mild, confiding eyes.

Such was she physically; he knew nothing of her spiritually, but only saw those eyes. And those eyes seemed to tell him all he needed to know. The meaning of their expression was this:

While still in the Institute, when she was fifteen, Liza used continually to fall in love with all the attractive men she met and was animated and happy only when she was in love. After leaving the Institute she continued to fall in love in just the same way with all the young men she met, and of course fell in love with Eugène as soon as she made his acquaintance. It was this being in love which gave her eyes that particular expression which so captivated Eugène. Already that winter she had been in love with two young men at one and the same time, and blushed and became excited not only when they entered the room but whenever their names were mentioned. But afterwards, when her mother hinted to her that Irtenev seemed to have serious intentions, her love for him increased so that she became almost indifferent to the two previous attractions, and when Irtenev began to come to their balls and parties and danced with her more than with others and evidently only wished to know whether she loved him, her love for him became painful. She dreamed of him in her sleep and seemed to see him when she was awake in a dark room, and everyone else vanished from her mind. But when he proposed and they were formally engaged, and when they had kissed one another and were a betrothed couple, then she had no thoughts but of him, no desire but to be with him, to love him, and to be loved by him. She was also proud of him and felt emotional about him and herself and her love, and quite melted and felt faint from love of him.

The more he got to know her the more he loved her. He had not at all expected to find such love, and it strengthened his own feeling still more.

VI

Towards spring he went to his estate at Semenovskoe to have a look at it and to give directions about the management, and especially about the house which was being done up for his wedding.

Mary Pavlovna was dissatisfied with her son's choice, not only because the match was not as brilliant as it might have been, but also because she did not like Varvara Alexeevna, his future mother-in-law. Whether she was good-natured or not she did not know and could not decide, but that she was not well-bred, not *comme il faut*—'not a lady' as Mary Pavlovna said to herself—she saw from their first acquaintance, and this distressed her; distressed her because she was accustomed to value breeding and knew that Eugène was alive to it, and she foresaw that he would suffer much annoyance on this account. But she liked the girl—liked her chiefly because Eugène did. One could not help loving her, and Mary Pavlovna was quite sincerely ready to do so.

Eugène found his mother contented and in good spirits. She was getting everything straight in the house and preparing to go away herself as soon as he brought his young wife. Eugène persuaded her to stay for the time being, and the future remained undecided.

In the evening after tea Mary Pavlovna played patience as usual. Eugène sat by, helping her. This was the hour of their most intimate talks. Having finished one game and while preparing to begin another, she looked up at him and, with a little hesitation, began thus:

'I wanted to tell you, Jenya—of course I don't know, but in general I wanted to suggest to you—that before your wedding it is absolutely necessary to have finished with all your bachelor affairs so that nothing may disturb either you or your wife. God forbid that it should. D'you follow me?'

Indeed Eugène at once understood that Mary Pavlovna was hinting at his relations with Stepanida which had ended in the previous autumn, and that she attributed much more importance to those relations than they deserved, as solitary women always do. Eugène blushed, not from shame so much as from vexation that good-natured Mary Pavlovna was bothering—out of affection no doubt, but still was bothering—about matters that were not her business and that she did not and could not understand. He answered that there was nothing that needed concealment, and that he had always conducted himself so that there should be nothing to hinder his marrying.

'Well, dear, that is excellent. Only, Jenya . . . don't be vexed with me,' said Mary Pavlovna, and broke off in confusion.

Eugène saw that she had not finished and had not said what she wanted to. And this was confirmed when a little later she began to tell him how, in his absence, she had been asked to stand godmother at . . . the Pechnikovs.

Eugène finished again, not with vexation or shame this time, but with some strange consciousness of the importance of what was about to be told him—an involuntary consciousness quite at variance with his conclusions. And what he expected happened. Mary Pavlovna, as if merely by way of conversation, mentioned that this year only boys were being born—evidently a sign of a coming war. Both at the Vasins and the Pechnikovs the young wife had a first child—at each house a boy. Mary Pavlovna wanted to say this casually, but she herself felt ashamed when she saw the colour mount to her son's face and saw him nervously removing, tapping, and replacing his pince-nez and hurriedly lighting a cigarette. She became silent. He too was silent and could not think how to break that silence. So they both understood that they had understood one another.

'Yes, the chief thing is that there should be justice and no favouritism in the village—as under your grandfather.'

'Mamma,' said Eugène suddenly, 'I know why you are saying this. You have no need to be disturbed. My, future family-life is so sacred to me that I should not infringe it in any case. And as to what occurred in my bachelor days, that is quite ended. I never formed any union and no one has any claims on me.'

'Well, I am glad,' said his mother. 'I know how noble your feelings are.'

Eugène accepted his mother's words as a tribute due to him, and did not reply.

Next day he drove to town thinking of his fiancée and of anything in the world except of Stepanida. But, as if purposely to remind him, on approaching the church he met people walking and driving back from it. He met old Matvey with Simon, some lads and girls, and then two women, one elderly, the other, who seemed familiar, smartly dressed and wearing a bright-red kerchief. This woman was walking lightly and boldly, carrying a child in her arms. He came up to them, and the elder woman bowed, stopping in the old-fashioned way, but the young woman with the child only bent her head, and from under the kerchief gleamed familiar, merry, smiling eyes.

Yes, this was she, but all that was over and it was no use looking at her: 'and the child may be mine,' flashed through his mind. No, what nonsense! There was her husband, she used to see him. He did not even consider the matter further, so settled in his mind was it that it had been necessary for his health—he had paid her money and there was no more to be said; there was, there had been, and there could be, no question of any union between them. It was not that he stifled the voice of conscience, no—his conscience simply said nothing to him. And he thought no more about her after the conversation with his mother and this meeting. Nor did he meet her again.

Eugène was married in town the week after Easter, and left at once with his young wife for his country estate. The house had been arranged as usual for a young couple. Mary Pavlovna wished to leave, but Eugène begged her to remain, and Liza still more strongly, and she only moved into a detached wing of the house.

And so a new life began for Eugène.

VII

The first year of his marriage was a hard one for Eugène. It was hard because affairs he had managed to put off during the time of his courtship now, after his marriage, all came upon him at once.

To escape from debts was impossible. An outlying part of the estate was sold and the most pressing obligations met, but others remained, and he had no money. The estate yielded a good revenue, but he had had to send payments to his brother and to spend on his own marriage, so that there was no ready money and the factory could not carry on and would have to be closed down. The only way of escape was to use his wife's money; and Liza, having realized her husband's situation, insisted on this herself. Eugène agreed, but only on condition that he should give her a mortgage on half his estate, which he did. Of course this was done not for his wife's sake, who felt offended at it, but to appease his mother-in-law.

These affairs with various fluctuations of success and failure helped to poison Eugène's life that first year. Another thing was his wife's ill-health. That same first year in autumn, seven months after their marriage, a misfortune befell Liza. She was driving out to meet her husband on his return from town, and the quiet horse became rather playful and she was frightened and jumped out. Her jump was comparatively fortunate—she might have been caught by the wheel—but she was pregnant, and that same night the pains began and she had a miscarriage from which she was long in recovering. The loss of the expected child and his wife's illness, together with the disorder in his affairs, and above all the presence of his mother-in-law, who arrived as soon as Liza fell ill—all this together made the year still harder for Eugène.

But notwithstanding these difficult circumstances, towards the end of the first year Eugène felt very fit. First of all his cherished hope of restoring his fallen fortune and renewing his grandfather's way of life in a new form, was approaching accomplishment, however slowly and with difficulty. There was no longer any question of having to sell the whole estate to meet the debts. The chief estate, though transferred to his wife's name, was saved, and if only the beet crop succeeded and the price kept up, by next year his position of want and stress might be replaced by one of relative prosperity. That was one thing.

Another was that however much he had expected from his wife, he had never expected to find in her what he actually found. He found not what he had expected, but something much better. Raptures of love—though he tried to produce them—did not take place or were very slight, but he discovered something quite different, namely, that he was not merely more cheerful and happier but that it had become easier to live. He did not know why this should be so, but it was.

And it was so because immediately after marriage his wife decided that Eugène Irtenev was superior to anyone else in the world: wiser, purer, and nobler than they, and that therefore it was right for everyone to serve him and please him; but that as it was impossible to make everyone do this, she must do it herself to the limit of her strength. And she did; directing all her strength of mind towards learning and guessing what he liked, and then doing just that thing, whatever it was and however difficult it might be.

She had the gift which furnishes the chief delight of intercourse with a loving woman: thanks to her love of her husband she penetrated into his soul. She knew his every state and his every shade of feeling—better it seemed to him than he himself—and she behaved correspondingly and therefore never hurt his feelings, but always lessened his distresses and strengthened his joys. And she understood not only his feelings but also his joys. Things quite foreign to her—concerning the farming, the factory, or the appraisement of others—she immediately understood so that she could not merely converse with him, but could often, as he himself said, be a useful and irreplaceable counsellor. She regarded affairs and people and everything in the world only through his eyes. She loved her mother, but having seen that Eugène disliked his mother-in-law's interference in their life she immediately took her husband's side, and did so with such decisiveness that he had to restrain her.

Besides all this she had very good taste, much tact, and above all repose. All that she did, she did unnoticed; only the results of what she did were observable, namely, that always and in everything there was cleanliness, order, and elegance. Liza had at once understood of what her husband's ideal of life consisted, and she tried to attain, and in the arrangement and order of the house did attain, what he wanted. Children it is true were lacking, but there was hope of that also. In winter she went to Petersburg to see a specialist and he assured them that she was quite well and could have children.

And this desire was accomplished. By the end of the year she was again pregnant.

The one thing that threatened, not to say poisoned, their happiness was her jealousy—a jealousy she restrained and did not exhibit, but from which she often suffered. Not only might Eugène not love any other woman—because there was not a woman on earth worthy of him (as to whether she herself was worthy or not she never asked herself)—but not a single woman might therefore dare to love him.

VIII

This was how they lived: he rose early, as he always had done, and went to see to the farm or the factory where work was going on, or sometimes to the fields. Towards ten o'clock he would come back for his coffee, which they had on the veranda: Mary Pavlovna, an uncle who lived with them, and Liza. After a conversation which was often very animated while they drank their coffee, they dispersed till dinner-time. At two o'clock they dined and then went for a walk or a drive. In the evening when he returned from his office they drank their evening tea and sometimes he read aloud while she worked, or when there were guests they had music or conversation. When he went away on business he wrote to his wife and received letters from her every day. Sometimes she accompanied him, and then they were particularly merry. On his name-day and on hers guests assembled, and it pleased him to see how well she managed to arrange things so that everybody enjoyed coming. He saw and heard that they all admired her—the young, agreeable hostess—and he loved her still more for this.

All went excellently. She bore her pregnancy easily and, though they were afraid, they both began making plans as to how they would bring the child up. The system of education and the arrangements were all decided by Eugène, and her only wish was to carry out his desires obediently. Eugène on his part read up medical works and intended to bring the child up according to all the precepts of science. She of course agreed to everything and made preparations, making warm and also cool 'envelopes', and preparing a cradle. Thus the second year of their marriage arrived and the second spring.

IX

It was just before Trinity Sunday. Liza was in her fifth month, and though careful she was still brisk and active. Both his mother and hers were living in the house, but under pretext of watching and safeguarding her only upset her by their tiffs. Eugène was specially engrossed with a new experiment for the cultivation of sugar-beet on a large scale.

Just before Trinity Liza decided that it was necessary to have a thorough house-cleaning as it had not been done since Easter, and she hired two women by the day to help the servants wash the floors and windows, beat the furniture and the carpets, and put covers on them. These women came early in the morning, heated the coppers, and set to work. One of the two was Stepanida, who had just weaned her baby boy and had begged for the job of washing the floors through the office-clerk—whom she now carried on with. She wanted to have a good look at the new mistress. Stepanida was living by herself as formerly, her husband being away, and she was up to tricks as she had formerly been first with old Daniel (who had once caught her taking some logs of firewood), afterwards with the master, and now with the young clerk. She was not concerning herself any longer about her master. 'He has a wife now,' she thought. But it would be good to have a look at the lady and at her establishment: folk said it was well arranged.

Eugène had not seen her since he had met her with the child. Having a baby to attend to she had not been going out to work, and he seldom walked through the village. That morning, on the eve of Trinity Sunday, he got up at five o'clock and rode to the fallow land which was to be sprinkled with phosphates, and had left the house before the women were about, and while they were still engaged lighting the copper fires.

He returned to breakfast merry, contented, and hungry; dismounting from his mare at the gate and handing her over to the gardener. Flicking the high grass with his whip and repeating a phrase he had just uttered, as one often does, he walked towards the house. The phrase was: 'phosphates justify'—what or to whom, he neither knew nor reflected.

They were beating a carpet on the grass. The furniture had been brought out.

'There now! What a house-cleaning Liza has undertaken! . . . Phosphates justify. . . . What a manageress she is! A manageress! Yes, a manageress,' said he to himself, vividly imagining her in her white wrapper and with her smiling joyful face, as it nearly always was when he looked at her. 'Yes, I must change my boots, or else "phosphates justify", that is, smell of manure, and the manageress is in such a condition. Why "in such a condition"?

Because a new little Irtenev is growing there inside her,' he thought. 'Yes, phosphates justify,' and smiling at his thoughts he put his hand to the door of his room.

But he had not time to push the door before it opened of itself and he came face to face with a woman coming towards him carrying a pail, barefoot and with sleeves turned up high. He stepped aside to let her pass and she too stepped aside, adjusting her kerchief with a wet hand.

'Go on, go on, I won't go in, if you . . .' began Eugène and suddenly stopped, recognizing her.

She glanced merrily at him with smiling eyes, and pulling down her skirt went out at the door.

'What nonsense! . . . It is impossible,' said Eugène to himself, frowning and waving his hand as though to get rid of a fly, displeased at having encountered her. He was vexed that he had noticed her and yet he could not take his eyes from her strong body, swayed by her agile strides, from her bare feet, or from her arms and shoulders, and the pleasing folds of her shirt and the handsome skirt tucked up high above her white calves.

'But why am I looking?' said he to himself, lowering his eyes so as not to see her. 'And anyhow I must go in to get some other boots.' And he turned back to go into his own room, but had not gone five steps before he again glanced round to have another look at her without knowing why or wherefore. She was just going round the corner and also glanced at him.

'Ah, what am I doing!' said he to himself. 'She may think . . . It is even certain that she already does think . . .'

He entered his damp room. Another woman, an old and skinny one, was there, and was still washing it. Eugène tiptoed across the floor, wet with dirty water, to the wall where his boots stood, and he was about to leave the room when the woman herself went out.

'This one has gone and the other, Stepanida, will come here alone,' someone within him began to reflect.

'My God, what am I thinking of and what am I doing!' He seized his boots and ran out with them into the hall, put them on there, brushed himself, and went out onto the veranda where both the mammas were already drinking coffee. Liza had evidently been expecting him and came onto the veranda through another door at the same time.

'My God! If she, who considers me so honourable, pure, and innocent—if she only knew!'—thought he.

Liza as usual met him with shining face. But today somehow she seemed to him particularly pale, yellow, long, and weak.

X

During coffee, as often happened, a peculiarly feminine kind of conversation went on which had no logical sequence but which evidently was connected in some way for it went on uninterruptedly.

The two old ladies were pin-pricking one another, and Liza was skilfully manoeuvring between them.

'I am so vexed that we hadn't finished washing your room before you got back,' she said to her husband. 'But I do so want to get everything arranged.'

'Well, did you sleep well after I got up?'

'Yes, I slept well and I feel fine.'

'How can a woman be fine in her condition during this intolerable heat, when her windows face the sun,' said Varvara Alexeevna, her mother. 'And they have no venetian blinds or awnings. I always had awnings.'

'But you know we are in the shade after ten o'clock,' said Mary Pavlovna.

'That's what causes fever; it comes of dampness,' said Varvara Alexeevna, not noticing that what she was saying did not agree with what she had just said. 'My doctor always says that it is impossible to diagnose an illness unless one knows the patient. And he certainly knows, for he is the leading physician and we pay him a hundred roubles a visit. My late husband did not believe in doctors, but he did not grudge me anything.'

'How can a man grudge anything to a woman when perhaps her life and the child's depend...'

'Yes, when she has means a wife need not depend on her husband. A good wife submits to her husband.' said Varvara Alexeevna—'only Liza is too weak after her illness.'

'Oh no, mamma, I feel quite well. But why have they not brought you any clotted cream?'

'I don't want any. I can do with raw cream.'

'I offered some to Varvara Alexeevna, but she declined,' said Mary Pavlovna, as if justifying herself.

'No, I don't want any today.' And as if to terminate an unpleasant conversation and yield magnanimously, Varvara Alexeevna turned to Eugène and said: 'Well, and have you sprinkled the phosphates?'

Liza ran to fetch the cream.

'But I don't want it. I don't want it.'

'Liza, Liza, go gently,' said Mary Pavlovna. 'Such rapid movements do her harm.'

'Nothing does harm if one's mind is at peace,' said Varvara Alexeevna as if referring to something, though she knew that there was nothing her words could refer to.

Liza returned with the cream and Eugène drank his coffee and listened morosely. He was accustomed to these conversations, but today he was particularly annoyed by its lack of sense. He wanted to think over what had happened to him but this chatter disturbed him. Having finished her coffee Varvara Alexeevna went away in a bad mood. Liza, Eugène, and Mary Pavlovna stayed behind, and their conversation was simple and pleasant. But Liza, being sensitive, at once noticed that something was tormenting Eugène, and she asked him whether anything unpleasant had happened. He was not prepared for this question and hesitated a little before replying that there had been nothing. This reply made Liza think all the more. That something was tormenting him, and greatly tormenting, was as evident to her as that a fly had fallen into the milk, yet he would not speak of it. What could it be?

XI

After breakfast they all dispersed. Eugène as usual went to his study, but instead of beginning to read or write his letters, he sat smoking one cigarette after another and thinking. He was terribly surprised and disturbed by the unexpected recrudescence within him of the bad feeling from which he had thought himself free since his marriage. Since then he had not once experienced that feeling, either for her—the woman he had known—or for any other woman except his wife. He had often felt glad of this emancipation, and now suddenly a chance meeting, seemingly so unimportant, revealed to him the fact that he was not free. What now tormented him was not that he was yielding to that feeling and desired her—he did not dream of so doing—but that the feeling was awake within him and he had to be on his guard against it. He had no doubt but that he would suppress it.

He had a letter to answer and a paper to write, and sat down at his writing-table and began to work. Having finished it and quite forgotten what had disturbed him, he went out to go to the stables. And again as ill-luck would have it, either by unfortunate chance or intentionally, as soon as he stepped from the porch a red skirt and red kerchief appeared from round the corner, and she went past him swinging her arms and swaying her body. She not only went past him, but on passing him ran, as if playfully, to overtake her fellow-servant.

Again the bright midday, the nettles, the back of Daniel's hut, and in the shade of the plane-trees her smiling face, biting some leaves, rose in his imagination.

'No, it is impossible to let matters continue so,' he said to himself, and waiting till the women had passed out of sight he went to the office.

It was just the dinner-hour and he hoped to find the steward still there, and so it happened. The steward was just waking up from his after-dinner nap, and stretching himself and yawning was standing in the office, looking at the herdsman who was telling him something.

'Vasili Nikolaich!' said Eugène to the steward.

'What is your pleasure?'

'I want to speak to you.'

'What is your pleasure?'

'Just finish what you are saying.'

'Aren't you going to bring it in?' said Vasili Nikolaich to the herdsman.

'It's heavy, Vasili Nikolaich.'

'What is it?' asked Eugène.

'Why, a cow has calved in the meadow. Well, all right, I'll order them to harness a horse at once. Tell Nicholas Lysukh to get out the dray cart.'

The herdsman went out.

'Do you know,' began Eugène, flushing and conscious that he was doing so, 'do you know, Vasili Nikolaich, while I was a bachelor I went off the track a bit. . . . You may have heard . . .'

Vasili Nikolaich, evidently sorry for his master, said with smiling eyes: 'Is it about Stepanida?'

'Why, yes. Look here. Please, please do not engage her to help in the house. You understand, it is very awkward for me . . .'

'Yes, it must have been Vanya the clerk who arranged it.'

'Yes, please . . . and hadn't the rest of the phosphates better be spread?' said Eugène, to hide his confusion.

'Yes, I am just going to see to it.'

So the matter ended, and Eugène calmed down, hoping that as he had lived for a year without seeing her, so things would go on now. 'Besides, Vasili Nikolaich will speak to Ivan the clerk; Ivan will speak to her, and she will understand that I don't want it,' said Eugène to himself, and he was glad that he had forced himself to speak to Vasili Nikolaich, hard as it had been to do so.

'Yes, it is better, much better, than that feeling of unease, that feeling of shame.' He shuddered at the mere remembrance of his sin in thought.

XII

The moral effort he had made to overcome his shame and speak to Vasili Nikolaich brought comfort to Eugène. It seemed to him that the matter was all over now. Liza at once noticed that he was quite calm, and even happier than usual. 'No doubt he was upset by our mothers pin-pricking one another. It really is disagreeable, especially for him who is so sensitive and noble, to keep on hearing such unfriendly and ill-mannered insinuations,' she thought.

The next day was Trinity Sunday. It was a beautiful day, and the peasant-women, on their way into the woods to plait wreaths, came according to custom to the landowner's home and began to sing and dance. Mary Pavlovna and Varvara Alexeevna came out onto the porch in smart clothes, carrying sunshades, and went up to the ring of singers. With them, in a jacket of Chinese silk, came out the uncle, a flabby libertine and drunkard, who was living that summer with Eugène.

As usual there was a bright, multi-coloured ring of young women and girls, the centre of everything, and around these from different sides like attendant planets that had detached themselves and were circling round, went girls hand in hand, rustling in their new print frocks; young lads giggling and running to and fro after one another; full-grown young fellows in dark blue or black coats and caps and with red shirts, who unceasingly spat out sunflower-seed husks; and the domestic servants or other outsiders watching the dance-circle from the edges. Both the old ladies went close up to the ring, and Liza accompanied them in a light blue dress, with light blue ribbons on her head, and wide sleeves beneath which her long white arms and angular elbows were visible.

Eugène had no wish to come out, but it was ridiculous to hide, and he too emerged onto the porch smoking a cigarette, bowed to the men and lads, and talked with one of them. The women meanwhile bawled a dance-song with all their might, snapping their fingers, clapping their hands, and dancing.

'They're calling for the master,' said a youngster coming up to Eugène's wife, who had not been aware of the summons. Liza called Eugène to look at the dance and at one of the women dancers who particularly pleased her. This was Stepanida. She wore a yellow skirt, a velveteen sleeveless jacket and a silk kerchief, and was broad, energetic, ruddy, and merry. No doubt she danced well. He saw nothing.

'Yes, yes,' he said, removing and replacing his pince-nez. 'Yes, yes,' he repeated. 'So it seems I cannot be rid of her,' he thought.

He did not look at her, fearing her attraction, and just on that account what his passing glance caught of her seemed to him especially alluring. Besides this he saw by her sparkling look that she saw him and saw that he admired her. He stood there as long as propriety demanded, and seeing that Varvara Alexeevna had called her 'my dear' senselessly and insincerely and was talking to her, he turned aside and went off.

He entered the house in order not to see her, but on reaching the upper storey he approached the window, without knowing how or why, and as long as the women remained at the porch he stood there and looked and looked at her, feasting his eyes on her.

He hurried down, while there was no one to see him, and then went silently onto the veranda, and from there, smoking a cigarette, he passed through the garden as if going for a stroll, following the direction she had taken. He had not gone two steps along the alley before he noticed behind the trees a velveteen sleeveless jacket, with a pink and yellow skirt and a red kerchief. She was going somewhere with another woman. 'Where are they going?'

And suddenly a terrible desire scorched him as though a hand were seizing his heart. As if by someone else's wish he looked round and went towards her.

'Eugène Ivanich, Eugène Ivanich! I have come to see your honour,' said a voice behind him, and Eugène, seeing old Samokhin who was digging a well for him, roused himself and turning quickly round went to meet Samokhin. While speaking with him he turned sideways and saw that she and the woman who was with her went down the slope, evidently to the well or making the well, a pretext to stop there a little while before running back to the dance-circle.

XIII

After talking to Samokhin, Eugène returned to the house as depressed as if he had committed a crime. In the first place she has read his mind, twigged that he wanted to see her, and desired it herself. Secondly, that other woman, Anna Prokhorova, evidently knew what was afoot.

Above all he felt that he was conquered, that he was not master of his own will but that there was another power moving him, that he had been saved only by good fortune, and that if not today then tomorrow or the next day, he would perish all the same.

'Yes, perish.' He did not understand it otherwise: to be unfaithful to his young and loving wife with a peasant-woman in the village, in the sight of everyone—what was it but to perish, perish utterly, so that it would be impossible to live? No, something must be done.

'My God, my God! What am I to do? Can it be that I shall perish like this?' he said to himself. 'Is it not possible to do anything? Yet something must be done. Do not think about her'—he ordered himself. 'Do not think!' and immediately he began thinking and seeing her before him, and seeing also the shade of the plane-tree.

He remembered having read of a hermit who, to avoid the temptation he felt for a woman on whom he had to lay his hand to heal her, thrust his other hand into a brazier and burned his fingers. He called that to mind. 'Yes, I am ready to burn my fingers rather than to perish.' He looked round to make sure that there was no one in the room, lit a candle, and put a finger into the flame. 'There, now think about her,' he said to himself ironically. It hurt him and he withdrew his smoke-stained finger, threw away the match, and laughed at himself. What nonsense! That was not what had to be done. But it was necessary to do something, to avoid seeing her—either to go away himself or to send her away. Yes—send her away. Offer her husband money to remove to town or to another village. People would hear of it and would talk about it. Well, what of that? At any rate it was better than this peril. 'Yes, that must be done,' he said to himself, and at that very moment he was looking at her without moving his eyes. 'Where is she going?' he suddenly asked himself. She, it seemed to him, had seen him at the window and now, having glanced at him and taken another woman by the hand, was going towards the garden swinging her arm briskly. Without knowing why or wherefore, merely in accord with what he had been thinking, he went to the office.

Vasili Nikolaich in holiday costume and with oiled hair was sitting at tea with his wife and a guest who was wearing an oriental kerchief.

'I want a word with you, Vasili Nikolaich!'

'Please say what you want to. We have finished tea.'

'No, I'd rather you came out with me.'

'Directly; only let me get my cap. Tanya, put out the samovar,' said Vasili Nikolaich, stepping outside cheerfully.

It seemed to Eugène that Vasili had been drinking, but what was to be done? It might be all the better—he would sympathize with him in his difficulties the more readily.

'I have come again to speak about that same matter, Vasili Nikolaich,' said Eugène—'about that woman.'

'Well, what of her? I told them not to take her again on any account.'

'No, I have been thinking in general, and this is what I wanted to take your advice about. Isn't it possible to get them away, to send the whole family away?'

'Where can they be sent?' said Vasili, disapprovingly and quizzically as it seemed to Eugène.

'Well, I thought of giving them money, or even some land in Koltovski—so that she should not be here.'

'But how can they be sent away? Where is he to go—torn from his roots? And why should you do it? What harm can she do you?'

'Ah, Vasili Nikolaich, you must understand that it would be dreadful for my wife to hear of it.'

'But who will tell her?'

'How can I live with this dread? The whole thing is very painful for me.'

'Really, why should you distress yourself? Whoever stirs up the past—out with his eye! Who is not a sinner before God and to blame before the Tsar, as the saying is?'

'All the same it would be better to get rid of them. Can't you speak to the husband?'

'But it's no use speaking! Eh, Eugène Ivanich, what's the matter with you? It's all past and forgotten. All sorts of things happen. Who is there that would now say anything bad of you? Everybody sees you.'

'But all the same go and have a talk with him.'

'All right, I will speak to him.'

Though he knew that nothing would come of it, this talk somewhat calmed Eugène. Mostly, it made him feel that through excitement he had been exaggerating the danger.

Had he gone to meet her by appointment? It was impossible. He had simply gone to stroll in the garden and she had happened to run out at the same time.

XIV

After dinner that very Trinity Sunday Liza while walking from the garden to the meadow, where her husband wanted to show her the clover, took a false step and fell when crossing a little ditch. She fell gently, on her side; but she gave an exclamation, and her husband saw an expression in her face not only of fear but of pain. He was about to help her up, but she motioned him away with her hand.

'No, wait a bit, Eugène,' she said, with a weak smile, and looked up guiltily as it seemed to him. 'My foot only gave way under me.'

'There, I always say,' remarked Varvara Alexeevna, 'can anyone in her condition possibly jump over ditches?'

'But it is all right, mama. I shall get up directly.' With her husband's help she did get up, but she immediately turned pale, and looked frightened.

'Yes, I am not all right!' and she whispered something to her mother.

'Oh, my God, what have you done! I said you ought not to go there,' cried Varvara Alexeevna. 'Wait—I will call the servants. She must not walk. She must be carried!'

'Don't be afraid, Liza, I will carry you,' said Eugène, putting his left arm round her. 'Hold me by the neck. Like that.' And stooping down he put his right arm under her knees and lifted her. He could never afterwards forget the suffering and yet beatific expression of her face.

'I am too heavy for you, dear,' she said with a smile. 'Mama is running—tell her!' And she bent towards him and kissed him. She evidently wanted her mother to see how he was carrying her.

Eugène shouted to Varvara Alexeevna not to hurry, and that he would carry Liza home. Varvara Alexeevna stopped and began to shout still louder.

'You will drop her, you'll be sure to drop her. You want to destroy her. You have no conscience!'

'But I am carrying her excellently.'

'I do not want to watch you killing my daughter, and I can't.' And she ran round the bend in the alley.

'Never mind, it will pass,' said Liza, smiling.

'Yes. If only it does not have consequences like last time.'

'No. I am not speaking of that. That's all right. I mean, mama—you are tired. Rest a bit.'

Though he found it heavy, Eugène carried his burden proudly and gladly to the house and did not hand her over to the housemaid and the chef whom Varvara Alexeevna had found and sent to meet them. He carried her to the bedroom and put her down on the bed.

'Now go away,' she said, and drawing his hand to her she kissed it. 'Annushka and I will manage all right.'

Mary Pavlovna also hurried in from her rooms in the wing. They undressed Liza and laid her on the bed. Eugène sat in the drawing-room with a book in his hand, waiting. Varvara Alexeevna went past him with such a reproachfully gloomy air that he felt alarmed.

'Well, how is it?' he asked.

'How is it? What's the good of asking? It is probably what you wanted when you made your wife jump over the ditch.'

'Varvara Alexeevna!' he cried. 'This is impossible. If you want to torment people and to poison their life . . .' (He wanted to continue: 'then go elsewhere to do it,' but restrained himself.) 'How is it that it does not hurt you?'

'It is too late now.' And shaking her cap in a triumphant manner she passed out by the door.

The fall had really been a bad one; Liza's foot had twisted awkwardly and there was danger of her having another miscarriage. Everyone knew that there was nothing to be done but that she must just lie quietly, yet all the same they decided to send for a doctor.

'Dear Nikolay Semenich,' wrote Eugène to the doctor, 'you have always been so kind to us that I hope you will not refuse to come to my wife's assistance. She . . .' and so on. Having written the letter he went to the stables to arrange about the horses and the carriage. Horses had to be got ready to bring the doctor and others to take him back. When an estate is not run on a large scale, such things cannot be quickly decided but have to be considered. Having arranged it all and dispatched the coachman, it was past nine before he got back to the house. His wife was lying down, and said that she felt perfectly well and had no pain. But Varvara Alexeevna was sitting with a lamp screened from Liza by some sheets of music and knitting a large red coverlet, with a mein that said that after what had happened peace was impossible, but that she at any rate would do her duty no matter what anyone else did.

Eugène noticed this, but, to appear as if he had not done so, tried to assume a cheerful and tranquil air and told how he had chosen the horses and how capitally the mare, Kabushka, had galloped as left trace-horse in the troika.

'Yes, of course, it's just the time to exercise the horses when help is needed. Probably the doctor will also be thrown into the ditch,' remarked Varvara Alexeevna, examining her knitting from under her pince-nez and moving it close up to the lamp.

'But you know we had to send one way or other, and I made the best arrangement I could.'

'Yes, I remember very well how your horses galloped with me under the arch of the gateway.' This was a long-standing fancy of hers, and Eugène now was injudicious enough to remark that that was not quite what had happened.

'It is not for nothing that I have always said, and have often remarked to the prince, that it is hardest of all to live with people who are untruthful and insincere. I can endure anything except that.'

'Well, if anyone has to suffer more than another, it is certainly I,' said Eugène. 'But you . . .'

'Yes, it is evident.'

'What?'

'Nothing, I am only counting my stitches.'

Eugène was standing at the time by the bed and Liza was looking at him, and one of her moist hands outside the coverlet caught his hand and pressed it. 'Bear with her for my sake. You know she cannot prevent our loving one another,' was what her look said.

'I won't do so again. It's nothing,' he whispered, and he kissed her damp, long hand and then her affectionate eyes, which closed while he kissed them.

'Can it be the same thing over again?' he asked. 'How are you feeling?'

'I am afraid to say for fear of being mistaken, but I feel that he is alive and will live,' said she, glancing at her stomach.

'Ah, it is dreadful, dreadful to think of.'

Notwithstanding Liza's insistence that he should go away, Eugène spent the night with her, hardly closing an eye and ready to attend on her.

But she passed the night well, and had they not sent for the doctor she would perhaps have got up.

By dinner-time the doctor arrived and of course said that if the symptoms recurred there might be cause for apprehension, yet actually there were no positive symptoms, but as there were also no contrary indications one might suppose on the one hand that—and on the other hand that . . . And therefore she must lie still, and that 'though I do not like prescribing, yet all the same she should take this mixture and should lie quiet.' Besides this, the doctor gave Varvara Alexeevna a lecture on woman's anatomy, during which Varvara Alexeevna nodded her head significantly. Having received his fee, as usual into the backmost part of his palm, the doctor drove away and the patient was left to lie in bed for a week.

XV

Eugène spent most of his time by his wife's bedside, talking to her, and what was hardest of all, enduring without murmur Varvara Alexeevna's attacks, and even contriving to turn these into jokes.

But he could not stay at home all the time. In the first place his wife sent him away, saying that he would fall ill if he always remained with her; and secondly the farming was progressing in a way that demanded his presence at every step. He could not stay at home, but had to be in the fields, in the wood, in the garden, at the threshing-floor; and everywhere he was pursued not merely by the thought but by the vivid image of Stepanida, and he only occasionally forgot her. But that would not have mattered, he could perhaps have mastered his feeling; the acute problem was that, whereas he had previously lived for months without seeing her, he now continually came across her. She evidently understood that he had the urge to renew relations with her and tried to come in his way. Nothing was said either by him or by her, and therefore neither he nor she went directly to a rendezvous, but only sought opportunities of meeting.

The most possible place for them to meet was in the forest, where peasant women went with sacks to collect grass for their cows. Eugène knew this and therefore went there every day. Every day he told himself that he would not go, and every day it ended by his making his way to the forest and, on hearing the sound of voices, standing behind the bushes with sinking heart looking to see if she was there.

Why he wanted to know whether it was she who was there, he did not know. If it had been she and she had been alone, he would not have gone to her—so he believed—he would have run away; but he wanted to see her.

Once he met her. As he was entering the forest she came out of it with two other women, carrying a heavy sack full of grass on her back. A little earlier he would perhaps have met her in the forest. Now, with the other women there, she could not go back to him. But though he realized this impossibility, he stood for a long time behind a hazelbush, at the risk of attracting the other women's attention. Of course she did not return, but he stayed there a long time. And, great heavens, how delightful his imagination made her appear to him! And this not only once, but five or six times, and each time more intensely. Never had she seemed so attractive, and never had he been so completely in her power.

He felt that he had lost control of himself and had become almost insane. His strictness with himself had not weakened a jot; on the contrary he saw all the abomination of his desire and even of his action, for his going to the wood was an action. He knew that he only need come near her anywhere in the dark, and if possible touch her, and he would yield to his feelings. He knew that it was only shame in the sight of others, and of her, and no doubt before himself also, that restrained him. And he knew too that he had sought conditions in which that shame would not be apparent—darkness or proximity—in which it would be stifled by animal passion. And therefore he knew that he was a wretched criminal, and despised and hated himself with all his soul. He hated himself because he still had not surrendered: every day he prayed God to strengthen him, to save him from perishing; every day he determined that from today onward he would not take a step to see her, and would forget her. Every day he devised means of delivering himself from this enticement, and made use of those means.

But it was all in vain.

One of the means was continual occupation; another was intense physical work and fasting; a third was imagining clearly to himself the disgrace that would fall upon him when everybody knew of it—his wife, his mother-in-law, and the folk around. He did all this and it seemed to him that he was conquering, but midday came—the hour of their former meetings and the hour when he had met her carrying the grass—and he would go to the forest. Thus five days of torment passed. He only saw her from a distance, and did not once encounter her.

XVI

Liza was gradually recovering, she could move about and was only uneasy at the change that had taken place in her husband, which she did not understand.

Varvara Alexeevna had gone away for a while, and the only visitor was Eugène's uncle. Mary Pavlovna was as usual at home.

Eugène was in his semi-insane condition when there came two days of pouring rain, as often happens after thunder in June. The rain stopped all work. They even ceased carting manure on account of the wet and dirt. The peasants stayed at home. The herdsmen wore themselves out with the cattle, and eventually drove them home. The cows and sheep wandered about in the pastureland and ran loose in the grounds. The peasant women, barefoot and wrapped in shawls, splashing through the mud, scurried about to seek the runaway cows. Streams flowed everywhere along the paths, all the leaves and all the grass were saturated, and streams flowed unceasingly from the spouts into the bubbling ponds.

Eugène sat at home with his wife, who was particularly wearisome that day. She questioned Eugène several times as to the cause of his discontent, and he replied with vexation that nothing was the matter. She ceased questioning him but was still distressed.

They were sitting after breakfast in the drawing-room. His uncle for the hundredth time was recounting fabrications about his society acquaintances. Liza was knitting a jacket and sighed, complaining of the weather and of a pain in the small of her back. The uncle advised her to lie down, and asked for vodka for himself. It was terribly tedious for Eugène in the house. Everything was weak and dull. He read a book and a magazine, but understood nothing of them.

'I must go out and look at the rasping-machine they brought yesterday,' he said, and got up and went out.

'Take an umbrella with you.'

'Oh, no, I have a leather coat. And I am only going as far as the boiling-room.'

He put on his boots and his leather coat and went to the factory; and he had not gone twenty steps before he met her coming towards him, with her skirts tucked up high above her white calves. She was walking, holding down the shawl in which her head and shoulders were wrapped.

'Where are you going?' he said, not recognizing her the first instant. When he did recognize her it was already too late. She Stopped, smiling, and looked long at him.

'I am looking for a calf. Where are you off to in such weather?' she said, as if she were seeing him every day.

'Come to the shed,' said he suddenly, without knowing how he said it. It was as if someone else had uttered the words.

She bit her shawl, winked, and ran in the direction which led from the garden to the shed, and he continued his path, intending to turn off beyond the lilac-bush and go there too.

'Master,' he heard a voice behind him. 'The mistress is calling you, and wants you to come back for a minute.'

This was Misha, his manservant.

'My God! This is the second time you have saved me,' thought Eugène, and immediately turned back. His wife reminded him that he had promised to take some medicine at the dinner-hour to a sick woman, and he had better take it with him.

While they were getting the medicine some five minutes elapsed, setting off with the medicine, he hesitated to go direct to the shed in case he should be seen from the house, but as soon as he was out of sight he promptly turned and made his way to it. He already saw her in imagination inside the shed smiling gaily. But she was not there, and there was nothing in the shed to show that she had been there.

He was already thinking that she had not come, had not heard or understood his words—he had muttered them through his nose as if afraid of her hearing them—or perhaps she had not wanted to come. 'And why did I imagine that she would rush to me? She has her own husband; it is only I who am such a wretch as to have a wife, and a good one, and to run after another.' Thus he thought sitting in the shed, the thatch of which had a leak and dripped from its straw. 'But how delightful it would be if she did come—alone here in this rain. If only I could embrace her once again, then let happen what may. But I could tell if she has been here by her footprints,' he reflected. He looked at the trodden ground near the shed and at the path overgrown by grass, and the fresh print of bare feet, and even of one that had slipped, was visible.

'Yes, she has been here. Well, now it is settled. Wherever I may see her I shall go straight to her. I will go to her at night.' He sat for a long time in the shed and left it exhausted and crushed. He delivered the medicine, returned home, and lay down in his room to wait for dinner.

XVII

Before dinner Liza came to him. Still wondering what could be the cause of his discontent, she began to say that she was afraid he did not like the idea of her going to Moscow for her confinement, and that she had decided that she would remain at home and on no account go to Moscow. He knew how she feared both her confinement itself and the risk of not having a healthy child, and therefore he could not help being touched at seeing how ready she was to sacrifice everything for his sake. All was so nice, so pleasant, so clean, in the house; and in his soul it was so dirty, despicable, and foul. The whole evening Eugène was tormented by knowing that notwithstanding his sincere repulsion at his own weakness, notwithstanding his firm intention to break off, the same thing would happen again tomorrow.

'No, this is impossible,' he said to himself, walking up and down in his room. 'There must be some remedy for it. My God! What am I to do?'

Someone knocked at the door, as foreigners do. He knew this must be his uncle. 'Come in,' he said.

The uncle had come as a self-appointed ambassador from Liza.

'Do you know, I really do notice that there is a change in you,' he said,—'and Liza—I understand how it troubles her. I understand that it must be hard for you to leave all the business you have so excellently started, but *que veux-tu*? I should advise you to go away. It will be more satisfactory both for you and for her. And do you know, I should advise you to go to the Crimea. The climate is beautiful and there is an excellent *accoucheur* there, and you would be just in time for the best of the grape season.'

'Uncle,' Eugène suddenly exclaimed. 'Can you keep a secret? A secret that is terrible to me, a shameful secret.'

'Oh, come—do you really feel any doubt of me?'

'Uncle, you can help me. Not only help, but save me!' said Eugène. And the thought of disclosing his secret to his uncle whom he did not respect, the thought that he would show himself in the worst light and humiliate himself before him, was pleasant. He felt himself to be despicable and guilty, and wished to punish himself.

'Speak, my dear fellow, you know how fond I am of you,' said the uncle, evidently well content that there was a secret and that it was a shameful one, and that it would be communicated to him, and that he could be of use.

'First of all I must tell you that I am a wretch, a good-for-nothing, a scoundrel—a real scoundrel.'

'Now what are you saying . . .' began his uncle, as if he were offended.

'What! Not a wretch when I—Liza's husband, Liza's! One has only to know her purity, her love—and that I, her husband, want to be untrue to her with a peasant-woman!'

'What is this? Why do you want to—you have not been unfaithful to her?'

'Yes, at least just the same as being untrue, for it did not depend on me. I was ready to do so. I was hindered, or else I should . . . now. I do not know what I would have done . . .'

'But please, explain to me . . .'

'Well, it is like this. When I was a bachelor I was stupid enough to have relations with a woman here in our village. That is to say, I used to have meetings with her in the forest, in the field . . .'

'Was she pretty?' asked his uncle.

Eugène frowned at this question, but he was in such need of external help that he made as if he did not hear it, and continued:

'Well, I thought this was just casual and that I should break it off and have done with it. And I did break it off before my marriage. For nearly a year I did not see her or think about her.' It seemed strange to Eugène himself to hear the description of his own condition. 'Then suddenly, I don't myself know why—really one sometimes believes in witchcraft—I saw her, and a worm crept into my heart; and it gnaws. I reproach myself, I understand the full horror of my action, that is to say, of the act I may commit any moment, and yet I myself turn to it, and if I have not committed it, it's only because God preserved me. Yesterday I was on my way to see her when Liza sent for me.'

'What, in the rain?'

'Yes. I am worn out, Uncle, and have decided to confess to you and to ask your help.'

'Yes, of course, it's a bad thing on your own estate. People will get to know. I understand that Liza is weak and that it is necessary to spare her, but why on your own estate?'

Again Eugène tried not to hear what his uncle was saying, and hurried on to the core of the matter.

'Yes, save me from myself. That is what I ask of you. Today I was hindered by chance. But tomorrow or next time no one will prevent me. And she knows now. Don't leave me alone.'

'Yes, all right,' said his uncle, 'but are you really so much in love?'

'Oh, it is not that at all. It's not that, it's some kind of power that has seized me and holds me. I don't know what to do. Perhaps I shall gain strength, and then ...'

'Well, it points to the advantage of what I suggested,' said his uncle. 'Let us be off to the Crimea.'

'Yes, yes, let's go, and meanwhile you will be with me and will talk to me.'

XVIII

The fact that Eugène had confided his secret to his uncle, and still more the sufferings of his conscience and the feeling of guilt he experienced after that rainy day, sobered him. It was settled that they would start for Yalta in a week's time. During that week Eugène drove to town to get money for the journey, gave instructions from the house and from the office concerning the management of the estate, again became cheerful and friendly with his wife, and began to awaken morally.

So without having once seen Stepanida after that rainy day he left with his wife for the Crimea. There he spent an excellent two months. He received so many new impressions that it seemed to him that the past was obliterated from his memory. In the

Crimea they met former acquaintances and became particularly friendly with them, and they also made new acquaintances. Life in the Crimea was a continual holiday for Eugène, besides being instructive and beneficial. They became friendly there with the former Marshal of the Nobility of their province, a clever and liberal-minded man who became fond of Eugène, took him under his wing, and attracted him to his Party.

At the end of August Liza gave birth to a beautiful, healthy daughter, and her confinement was unexpectedly easy.

In September they returned home, the four of them, including the baby and its wet-nurse, as Liza was unable to feed it herself. Eugène returned home entirely free from the former horrors and quite a new and happy man. Having gone through all that a husband goes through when his wife bears a child, he loved her more than ever. His feeling for the child when he took it in his arms was a funny, new, very pleasant and kind of tickling feeling. Another new thing in his life now was that, besides his occupation with the estate, thanks to his acquaintance with Dumchin, the ex-Marshal, a new interest occupied his mind, that of the Zemstvo—partly an ambitious interest, partly a sense of duty. In October there was to be a special Assembly, at which he was to be elected. After arriving home he drove once to town and another time to Dumchin.

Of the torments of his temptation and struggle he had forgotten even to think, and only with difficulty could recall them to mind. It seemed to him that he had undergone something like an attack of insanity.

To such an extent did he now feel free from it that he was not even afraid to make inquiries at the first opportunity when he was alone with the steward. Since he had previously spoken to him about the matter he was not shy at asking.

'Well, and is Sidor Pechnikov still away from home?' he inquired.

'Yes, he is still in Town.'

'And his wife?'

'Oh, she is a worthless woman. She's now carrying on with Zenovi. She has gone quite on the loose.'

'Well, that's all right,' thought Eugène. 'How wonderfully indifferent to it I am! How I have changed.'

XIX

All that Eugène had wished had been realized. He had obtained the property, the factory was working successfully, the beet-crops were excellent, and he expected a large income; his wife had borne a child satisfactorily, his mother-in-law had left, and he had been unanimously elected to the Zemstvo.

He was returning home from town after the election. He had been congratulated and had had to return thanks. He had had dinner and had drunk some five glasses of champagne. Quite new plans of life now presented themselves to him, and he was thinking about these as he drove home. It was an Indian summer: an excellent road and a hot sun. As he approached his home Eugène was thinking of how, as a result of this election, he would occupy among the people the position he had always dreamed of; that is to say, one in which he would be able to serve them not only by production, which gave employment, but also by direct influence. He imagined what his own and the other peasants would think of him in three years' time. 'For instance this one,' he thought, driving just then through the village and glancing at a peasant who with a peasant woman was crossing the street in front of him carrying a full water-tub. They stopped to let his carriage pass. The peasant was old Pechnikov, and the woman was Stepanida. Eugène looked at her, recognized her, and was glad to feel that he remained quite unmoved. She was still as good-looking as ever, but this did not touch him at all. He drove home.

'Well, may we congratulate you?' said his uncle.

'Yes, I was elected.'

'Capital! We must drink to it!'

Next day Eugène drove about to see to the farming which he had been neglecting. At the outlying farmstead a new threshing machine was at work. While watching it Eugène stepped among the women, trying not to take notice of them; but try as he would he once or twice noticed the black eyes and red kerchief of Stepanìda, who was carrying away the straw. Once or twice he glanced sideways at her and felt that something was happening, but could not account for it to himself. Only next day, when he again drove to the threshing-floor and spent two hours there quite unnecessarily, without ceasing to caress with his eyes the familiar, handsome figure of the young women, did he feel that he was lost, irremediably lost. Again those torments! Again all that horror and fear, and there was no saving himself.

What he expected happened to him. The evening of the next day, without knowing how, he found himself at her back-yard, by her hay-shed, where in autumn they had once had an assignation. As though having a stroll, he stopped there lighting a cigarette. A neighbouring peasant woman saw him, and as he turned back he heard her say to someone: 'Go, he is waiting for you—on my dying word he is standing there. Go, you fool!'

He saw how a woman—she—ran to the hay-shed; but since a peasant had met him it was no longer possible for him to turn back, and so he went home.

XX

When he entered the drawing-room everything seemed strange and unnatural to him. He had risen that morning vigorous, determined to fling it all aside, to forget it and not allow himself to think about it. But without noticing how it occurred he had all the morning not merely not interested himself in the work in hand, but tried to avoid it. What had formerly cheered him and been important was now insignificant. Unconsciously he tried to free himself from business. It seemed to him that he had to do so in order to think and to plan. And, indeed, he freed himself and remained alone. But as soon as he was alone he began to wander about in the garden and the woods. And all those spots were tainted in his recollection by memories that gripped him. He felt that he was walking in the garden and pretending to himself that he was thinking out something, yet really he was not thinking out anything but insanely and irrationally expecting her; expecting that by some miracle she would be aware that he was expecting her, and would come here at once and go somewhere where no one would see them, or would come at night when there would be no moon, and no one, not even she herself, would see—on such a night she would come and he would touch her body . . .

'There now, talking of breaking off when I wish to,' said he to himself. 'And having a clean healthy woman for one's health sake! One can't play with her like that. I thought I had taken her, but it was she who took me; took me and does not let me go. Why, I thought I was free, but I wasn't free and was deceiving myself when I married. It was all nonsense—fraud. From the time I had her I experienced a new feeling—the real feeling of a husband. I ought to have lived with her.

'One of two lives is possible for me: that which I began with Liza: service, estate management, the child, and people's respect. If that is life, it's necessary that she, Stepanida, should not be there. She must be sent away, as I said, or destroyed so that she shall not exist. And the other life—is this: For me to take her away from her husband, pay him money, disregard the shame and disgrace, and live with her. But in that case it is necessary that Liza should not exist, nor Mimi (the baby). No, that's not so: the baby doesn't matter, but it *is* necessary that there should be no Liza—that she should be gone—that she should know, curse me, and go away. That she should know that I have exchanged her for a peasant-woman, that I am a deceiver and a scoundrel!—No, that's too terrible! It's impossible. Yet it might happen,' he went on thinking,—'it might happen that Liza might fall ill and die. Die, and then everything would be capital.

'Capital! Oh, scoundrel! No, if someone must die it should be Stepanida. If she were to die, how good it would be.

'Yes, that is how men come to poison or kill their wives or lovers. Take a revolver and go and call her, and instead of embracing her, shoot her in the breast and have done with it.

'Really she is—a devil. Simply a devil. She has possessed herself of me against my own will.

'To kill, yes. There are only two way out: to kill my wife, or to kill her. For it is impossible to live like this,' said he to himself, and going up to the table he took from it a revolver and, having examined it—one cartridge was wanting—he put it in his trouser pocket.

'My God! What am I doing?' he suddenly exclaimed, and folding his hands he began to pray.

'O God, help me and deliver me! Thou knowest that I do not desire evil, but by myself am powerless. Help me,' said he, making the sign of the cross on his breast before the icon.

'Yes, I can control myself. I will go out, walk about and think things over.'

He went to the entrance-hall, put on his overcoat and went out onto the porch. Unconsciously his steps took him past the garden along the field path to the outlying farmstead. There the threshing machine was still droning and the cries of the driver-lads were heard. He entered the barn. She was there. He saw her at once. She was raking up the corn, and on seeing him she ran briskly and merrily about, with laughing eyes, raking up the scattered corn with agility. Eugène could not help watching her though he did not wish to do so. He only recollected himself when she was no longer in sight. The clerk informed him that they were now finishing threshing the corn that had been beaten down—that was why it was going slower and the output was less. Eugène went up to the drum, which occasionally gave a knock as sheaves not evenly fed in passed under it, and he asked the clerk if there were many such sheaves of beaten-down corn.

'There will be five cartloads of it.'

'Then look here . . .' began Eugène, but he did not finish the sentence, She had gone close up to the drum and was raking the corn from under it, and she scorched him with her laughing eyes. That look spoke of a merry, careless love between them, of the fact that she knew he wanted her and had come to her shed, and that she as always was ready to live and be merry with him regardless of all conditions or consequences. Eugène felt himself to be in her power yet did not wish to yield.

He remembered his prayer and tried to repeat it. He began saying it to himself, but at once felt that it was useless. A single thought now engrossed him entirely: how to arrange a meeting with her so that others would not be aware of it.

'If we finish this lot today, are we to start on a fresh stack or leave it till tomorrow?' asked the clerk.

'Yes, yes,' replied Eugène, involuntarily following her to the heap to which with the other women she was raking the corn.

'But can I really not master myself?', he was saying to himself. 'Have I really perished? O God! But there is no God. There is only a devil. And it is she, She has possessed me. But I won't, I won't! A devil, yes, a devil.'

Again he went up to her, drew the revolver from his pocket and shot her, once, twice, thrice, in the back. She ran a few steps and fell on the heap of corn.

'My God, my God! What is that?' cried the women.

'No, it was not an accident. I killed her on purpose,' cried Eugène. 'Send for the policeman.'

He went home and entered his study, locking himself in without speaking to his wife.

'Do not come to me,' he called to her through the door. 'You will know all about it.'

An hour later he rang, and bade the man-servant who answered the bell: 'Go and find out whether Stepanida is alive.'

The servant already knew all about it, and told him she had died an hour ago.

'Well, all right. Now leave me alone. When the policeman or the magistrate comes, let me know.'

The police officer and magistrate arrived next morning, and Eugène, having bidden his wife and baby farewell, was taken to prison.

He was tried. It was during the early days of trial by jury, and the verdict was one of temporary insanity. He was sentenced only to perform church penance.

He had been kept in prison for nine months and was then confined in a monastery for one month.

He had begun to drink while still in prison, continued to do so in the monastery, and returned home an enfeebled, feckless drunkard.

Varvara Alexeevna assured them that she had always predicted this. It was, she said, evident from the way he argued. Neither Liza nor Mary Pavlovna could understand how the affair had happened, but for all that, they did not believe what the doctors said, namely, that he was mentally deranged—a psychopath. They could not accept that, for they knew that he was saner than hundreds of their acquaintances.

And indeed, if Eugène Irtenev was mentally deranged when he committed this crime, then everyone is similarly insane. The most mentally deranged people are certainly those who see in others indications of insanity they do not discern in themselves.

The Kreutzer Sonata
[1889]

But I say unto you, that every one that looketh on a woman to lust after her hath committed adultery with her already in his heart. Matt. v. 28.

The disciples say unto him, If the case of the man is so with his wife, it is not expedient to marry. But he said unto them, All men cannot receive this saying, but they to whom it is given. Ibid. xix. 10, 11.

I

It was early spring, and the second day of our journey. Passengers going short distances entered and left our carriage, but three others, like myself, had come all the way with the train. One was a lady, plain and no longer young, who smoked, had a harassed look, and wore a mannish coat and cap; another was an acquaintance of hers, a talkative man of about forty, whose things looked neat and new; the third was a rather short man who kept himself apart. He was not old, but his curly hair had gone prematurely grey. His movements were abrupt and his unusually glittering eyes moved rapidly from one object to another. He wore an old overcoat, evidently from a first-rate tailor, with an astrakhan collar, and a tall astrakhan cap. When he unbuttoned his overcoat a sleeveless Russian coat and embroidered shirt showed beneath it. A peculiarity of this man was a strange sound he emitted, something like a clearing of his throat, or a laugh begun and sharply broken off.

All the way this man had carefully avoided making acquaintance or making any intercourse with his fellow passengers. When spoken to by those near him he gave short and abrupt answers, and at other times read, looked out of the window, smoked, or drank tea and ate something he took out of an old bag.

It seemed to me that his loneliness depressed him, and I made several attempts to converse with him, but whenever our eyes met, which happened often as he sat nearly opposite me, he turned away and took up his book or looked out of the window.

Towards the second evening, when our train stopped at a large station, this nervous man fetched himself some boiling water and made tea. The man with the neat new things—a lawyer as I found out later—and his neighbour, the smoking lady with the mannish coat, went to the refreshment-room to drink tea.

During their absence several new passengers entered the carriage, among them a tall, shaven, wrinkled old man, evidently a merchant, in a coat lined with skunk fur, and a cloth cap with an enormous peak. The tradesman sat down opposite the seats of the lady and the lawyer, and immediately started a conversation with a young man who had also entered at that station and, judging by his appearance, was a merchant's clerk.

I was sitting the other side of the gangway and as the train was standing still I could hear snatches of their conversation when nobody was passing between us. The merchant began by saying that he was going to his estate which was only one station farther on; then as usual the conversation turned to prices and trade, and they spoke of the state of business in Moscow and then of the Nizhni-Novgorod Fair. The clerk began to relate how a wealthy merchant, known to both of them, had gone on the spree at the fair, but the old man interrupted him by telling of the orgies he had been at in former times at Kunavin Fair. He evidently prided himself on the part he had played in them, and recounted with pleasure how he and some acquaintances, together with the merchant they had been speaking of, had once got drunk at Kunavin and played such a trick that he had to tell of it in a whisper. The clerk's roar of laughter filled the whole carriage; the old man laughed also, exposing two yellow teeth.

Not expecting to hear anything interesting, I got up to stroll about the platform till the train should start. At the carriage door I met the lawyer and the lady who were talking with animation as they approached.

'You won't have time,' said the sociable lawyer, 'the second bell will ring in a moment.'

And the bell did ring before I had gone the length of the train. When I returned, the animated conversation between the lady and the lawyer was proceeding. The old tradesman sat silent opposite to them, looking sternly before him, and occasionally mumbled disapprovingly as if chewing something.

'Then she plainly informed her husband,' the lawyer was smilingly saying as I passed him, 'that she was not able, and did not wish, to live with him since . . .'

He went on to say something I could not hear. Several other passengers came in after me. The guard passed, a porter hurried in, and for some time the noise made their voices inaudible. When all was quiet again the conversation had evidently turned from the particular case to general considerations.

The lawyer was saying that public opinion in Europe was occupied with the question of divorce, and that cases of 'that kind' were occurring more and more often in Russia. Noticing that his was the only voice audible, he stopped his discourse and turned to the old man.

'Those things did not happen in the old days, did they?' he said, smiling pleasantly.

The old man was about to reply, but the train moved and he took off his cap, crossed himself, and whispered a prayer. The lawyer turned away his eyes and waited politely. Having finished his prayer and crossed himself three times the old man set his cap straight, pulled it well down over his forehead, changed his position, and began to speak.

'They used to happen even then, sir, but less often,' he said. 'As times are now they can't help happening. People have got too educated.'

The train moved faster and faster and jolted over the joints of the rails, making it difficult to hear, but being interested I moved nearer. The nervous man with the glittering eyes opposite me, evidently also interested, listened without changing his place.

'What is wrong with education?' said the lady, with a scarcely perceptible smile. 'Surely it can't be better to marry as they used to in the old days when the bride and bridegroom did not even see one another before the wedding,' she continued, answering not what her interlocutor had said but what she thought he would say, in the way many ladies have. 'Without knowing whether they loved, or whether they could love, they married just anybody, and were wretched all their lives. And you think that was better?' she said, evidently addressing me and the lawyer chiefly and least of all the old man with whom she was talking.

'They've got so very educated,' the merchant reiterated, looking contemptuously at the lady and leaving her question unanswered.

'It would be interesting to know how you explain the connection between education and matrimonial discord,' said the lawyer, with a scarcely perceptible smile.

The tradesman was about to speak, but the lady interrupted him.

'No,' she said, 'those times have passed.' But the lawyer stopped her.

'Yes, but allow the gentleman to express his views.'

'Foolishness comes from education,' the old man said categorically.

'They make people who don't love one another marry, and then wonder that they live in discord,' the lady hastened to say, turning to look at the lawyer, at me, and even at the clerk, who had got up and, leaning on the back of the seat, was smilingly listening to the conversation. 'It's only animals, you know, that can be paired off as their master likes; but human beings have their own inclinations and attachments,' said the lady, with an evident desire to annoy the tradesman.

'You should not talk like that, madam,' said the old man, 'animals are cattle, but human beings have a law given them.'

'Yes, but how is one to live with a man when there is no love?' the lady again hastened to express her argument, which probably seemed very new to her.

'They used not to go into that,' said the old man in an impressive tone. 'It is only now that all this has sprung up. The least thing makes them say: "I will leave you!" The fashion has spread even to the peasants. "Here you are!" she says. "Here, take your shirts and trousers and I will go with Vanka; his head is curlier than yours." What can you say? The first thing that should be required of a woman is fear!'

The clerk glanced at the lawyer, at the lady, and at me, apparently suppressing a smile and prepared to ridicule or to approve of the merchant's words according to the reception they met with.

'Fear of what?' asked the lady.

'Why this: Let her fear her husband! That fear!'

'Oh, the time for that, sir, has passed,' said the lady with a certain viciousness.

'No, madam, that time cannot pass. As she, Eve, was made from the rib of a man, so it will remain to the end of time,' said the old man, jerking his head with such sternness and such a victorious look that the clerk at once concluded that victory was on his side, and laughed loudly.

'Ah yes, that's the way you men argue,' said the lady unyieldingly, and turned to us. 'You have given yourselves freedom but want to shut women up in a tower. You no doubt permit yourselves everything.'

'No one is permitting anything, but a man does not bring offspring into the home; while a woman—a wife—is a leaky vessel,' the tradesman continued insistently. His tone was so impressive that it evidently vanquished his hearers, and even the lady felt crushed but still did not give in.

'Yes, but I think you will agree that a woman is a human being and has feelings as a man has. What is she to do then, if she does not love her husband?'

'Does not love!' said the tradesman severely, moving his brows and lips. 'She'll love, no fear!' This unexpected argument particularly pleased the clerk, and he emitted a sound of approval.

'Oh, no, she won't!' the lady began. 'And when there is no love you can't enforce it.'

'Well, and supposing the wife is unfaithful, what then?' asked the lawyer.

'That is not admissible,' said the old man. 'One has to see to that.'

'But if it happens, what then? You know it does occur.'

'It happens among some, but not among us,' said the old man.

All were silent. The clerk moved, came still nearer, and, evidently unwilling to be left out, began with a smile.

'Yes, a young fellow of ours had a scandal. It was a difficult case to deal with. It too was a case of a woman who was a bad lot. She began to play the devil, and the young fellow is respectable and cultured. At first it was with one of the office-workers. The husband tried to persuade her with kindness. She would not stop, but played all sorts of dirty tricks. Then she began to steal his money. He beat her, but she only grew worse. Carried on intrigues, if I may mention it, with an unchristened Jew. What was he to do? He turned her out altogether and lives as a bachelor, while she gads about.'

'Because he is a fool,' said the old man. 'If he'd pulled her up properly from the first and not let her have her way, she'd be living with him, no fear! It's giving way at first that counts. Don't trust your horse in the field, or your wife in the house.'

At that moment the guard entered to collect the tickets for the next station. The old man gave up his.

'Yes, the female sex must be curbed in good time or else all is lost!'

'Yes, but you yourself just now were speaking about the way married men amuse themselves at the Kunavin Fair,' I could not help saying.

'That's a different matter,' said the old man and relapsed into silence.

When the whistle sounded the tradesman rose, got out his bag from under the seat, buttoned up his coat, and slightly lifting his cap went out of the carriage.

II

As soon as the old man had gone several voices were raised.

'A stickler of the old school!' remarked the clerk.

'The embodiment of a domestic tyrant' said the lady. 'What barbarous views of women and marriage!'

'Yes, we are still a long way from the European understanding of marriage,' said the lawyer.

'The chief thing such people do not understand,' continued the lady, 'is that marriage without love is not marriage; that love alone sanctifies marriage, and that real marriage is only such as is sanctified by love.'

The clerk listened smilingly, trying to store up for future use all he could of the clever conversation.

In the midst of the lady's remarks we heard, behind me, a sound like that of a broken laugh or sob; and on turning round we saw my neighbour, the lonely grey-haired man with the glittering eyes, who had approached unnoticed during our conversation, which evidently interested him. He stood with his arms on the back of the seat, evidently much excited; his face was quite flushed and a muscle twitched in his cheek.

'What kind of love . . . love . . . is it that sanctifies marriage?' he asked hesitatingly.

Noticing the speaker's agitation, the lady tried to answer him as gently and fully as possible.

'True love . . . When such love exists between a man and a woman, then marriage is possible,' she said.

'Yes, but how is one to understand what is meant by "true love"?' said the gentleman with the glittering eyes timidly and with an awkward smile.

'Everybody knows what love is,' replied the lady, evidently wishing to bring this conversation to a close.

'But I don't,' said the man. 'You must define what you understand . . .'

'Why? It's very simple,' she said, but stopped to consider. 'Love? Love is an exclusive preference for one above everybody else,' said the lady.

'Preference for how long? A month, two days, or half an hour?' said the grey-haired man and began to laugh.

'Excuse me, we are evidently not speaking of the same thing.'

'Oh, yes! Exactly the same.'

'She means,' interposed the lawyer, pointing to the lady, 'that in the first place marriage must be the outcome of attachment—or love, if you please—and only where that exists is marriage sacred, so to speak. Secondly, that marriage when not based on natural attachment—love, if you prefer the word—lacks the element that makes it morally binding. Do I understand you rightly?' he added, addressing the lady.

The lady indicated her approval of his explanation by a nod of her head.

'It follows . . .' the lawyer continued—but the nervous man whose eyes now glowed as if aflame and who had evidently restrained himself with difficulty, began without letting the lawyer finish:

'Yes, I mean exactly the same thing, a preference for one person over everybody else, and I am only asking: a preference for how long?'

'For how long? For a long time; for life sometimes,' replied the lady, shrugging her shoulders.

'Oh, but that happens only in novels and never in real life. In real life this preference for one may last for years (that happens very rarely), more often for months, or perhaps for weeks, days, or hours,' he said, evidently aware that he was startling everybody by his views and pleased that it was so.

'Oh, what are you saying?' 'But no . . .' 'Sorry, no . . .' we all three began at once. Even the clerk uttered an imprecise sound of disapproval.

'I know, I know,' the grey-haired man shouted above our voices—'you're talking about what is supposed to be, but I am speaking about what actually happens. Every man experiences what you call love for every pretty woman.'

'Oh, what you say is awful! But the feeling that is called love does exist among people, and is given not for months or years, but for a lifetime!'

'No, it does not! Even if we can grant that a man might prefer a certain woman all his life, the woman in all probability would prefer someone else. It's the way it always has been and still is in the world,' he said, and taking out his cigarette-case he began to smoke.

'But the feeling may be reciprocal,' said the lawyer.

'No, sir, it can't!' rejoined the other. 'Just as it cannot be that in a cartload of peas, two marked peas will lie side by side. Besides, it is not merely this impossibility, but the inevitable satiety. To love one person for a whole lifetime is like saying that one candle will burn a whole life,' he said, greedily inhaling the smoke.

'But you are talking all the time about physical love. Don't you acknowledge love based on identity of ideals, on spiritual affinity?' asked the lady.

'Spiritual affinity! Identity of ideals!' he repeated, emitting his peculiar sound. 'But in that case why go to bed together? (Excuse my coarseness!) Or do people go to bed together because of the identity of their ideals?' he said, breaking into a nervous laugh.

'But permit me,' said the lawyer. 'Facts contradict you. We do see that matrimony exists, that all mankind, or the greater part of it, lives in wedlock, and many people honourably live long married lives.'

The grey-haired man again laughed.

'First you say that marriage is based on love, and when I express a doubt as to the existence of a love other than sensual, you prove the existence of love by the fact that marriages exist. but marriages in our days are mere deception!'

'No, allow me!' said the lawyer. 'I only say that marriages have existed and do exist.'

'They do! But why? They have existed and do exist among people who see in marriage something sacramental, a mystery binding them in the sight of God. Among them marriages do exist. Among us, people marry regarding marriage as nothing but copulation, and the result is either deception or coercion. When it is deception it is easier to bear. The husband and wife merely deceive people by pretending to be monogamists, while living polygamously. That is bad, but still bearable. But when, as most frequently happens, the husband and wife have accepted the obligation of living together all their lives, and have begun to hate each other after a month, longing to part but still continuing to live together, it leads to that terrible hell which makes people take to drink, shoot themselves, and kill or poison themselves or one another,' he went on, speaking more and more rapidly, not allowing anyone to put in a word and becoming more and more excited. We all felt embarrassed.

'Yes, undoubtedly there are critical episodes in married life,' said the lawyer, wishing to end this disturbingly heated conversation.

'I see you have found out who I am!' said the grey-haired man softly, and with apparent calm.

'No, I have not that pleasure.'

'It is no great pleasure. I am that Pozdnyshev in whose life just such a critical episode occurred to which you alluded; the episode ending with the killing of my wife,' he said, rapidly glancing at each of us.

No one knew what to say and all remained silent.

'Well, never, mind,' he said with that peculiar sound of his. 'However, pardon me. Ah! . . . I don't want to embarrass you.'

'Oh, no, by no means . . .' said the lawyer, himself not knowing 'by no means' what.

But Pozdnyshev, without listening to him, rapidly turned away and went back to his seat. The lawyer and the lady whispered together. I sat down beside Pozdnyshev in silence, unable to think of anything to say. It was too dark to read, so I shut my eyes pretending that I wished to go to sleep. So we travelled in silence to the next station.

At that station the lawyer and the lady moved into another carriage, having some time previously had a word with the guard about it. The clerk lay down on the seat and fell asleep. Pozdnyshev kept smoking and drinking tea which he had made at the last station.

When I opened my eyes and looked at him he suddenly addressed me resolutely and irritably:

'Perhaps it is unpleasant for you to sit with me, knowing who I am? In that case I'll move off.'

'Oh no, not at all.'

'Well then, won't you have some? Only it's very strong.'

He poured out some tea for me.

'They talk . . . and always they lie . . .' he remarked.

'What are you speaking about?' I asked.

'Always about the same thing. About that love of theirs and what it is! Don't you want to sleep?'

'Not at all.'

'Then would you like me to tell you how that love led to what happened to me?'

'—if it will not be painful for you.'

'No, it's painful for me to be silent. Drink the tea . . . or is it too strong?'

The tea was really like beer, but I drank a glass of it. Just then the guard entered. Pozdnyshev followed him with hostile eyes, and only began to speak after he had left.

III

'Well then, I'll tell you. But do you really want to hear it?'

I repeated that I wished it very much. He paused, rubbed his face with his hands, and began:

'If I am to tell it, I must tell everything from the beginning: I must tell how and why I married, and the kind of man I was before my marriage.

'Up to my marriage I lived as everybody does, that is, everybody in our class. I'm a landowner and a university graduate, and was a marshal of the gentry. Before my marriage I lived as everyone does, that is, dissolutely; and while living dissolutely I was convinced, like everybody in our class, that I was living as one has to. I thought I was a charming fellow and quite a moral man. I was not a seducer, had no unnatural tastes, did not make that the chief purpose of my life as many of my associates did, but I practised debauchery in a steady, decent way for health's sake. I avoided women who might tie my hands by having a child or by attachment for me. If there may have been children and attachments, but I acted as if there were not. And this I not only considered moral: I was even proud of it.'

He paused and gave vent to that peculiar sound, which he evidently did whenever a new idea occurred to him.

'And you know, that's the chief abomination!' he exclaimed. 'Dissoluteness does not lie in anything physical—no kind of physical misconduct is debauchery; real debauchery lies precisely in freeing oneself from moral relations with a woman with whom you have physical intimacy. And such emancipation I regarded as a merit. I remember how I once worried because I hadn't had an opportunity to pay a woman who gave herself to me (having probably taken a fancy to me) and how I only regained my usual serenity after having sent her some money—thereby intimating that I did not consider myself in any way morally bound to her ... Don't nod as if you agreed with me,' he suddenly exclaimed. 'Don't I know these things? We all, and you too unless you are a rare exception, hold those same views, just as I used to. Forgive me, but the fact is that all this is terrible, terrible, terrible!'

'What is terrible?' I asked.

'That abyss of error in which we live concerning women and our relations with them. No, I can't speak calmly about it, not because of that "episode," in my life, but because since that "episode" occurred my eyes have been opened and I have seen everything in quite a different light. Everything turned inside out, yes inside out!'

He lit a cigarette and began to speak, leaning his elbows on his knees.

It was too dark to see his face, but, above the jolting of the train, I could hear his impressive and pleasant voice.

IV

'Yes, only after such torments as I have endured, only by means of them, have I understood where the root of the matter lies—understood what ought to be, and therefore seen all the horror of what is.

'So you will see how and when that which led up to my "episode" began. It began when I was not quite sixteen. It happened when I was still going to grammar school and my elder brother was a first-year student at the university. I had not yet known any woman, but, like all the unfortunate children of our class, I was no longer an innocent boy. I had been depraved two years before that by other boys. Already woman, not some particular woman but woman as something to be desired, woman, every woman, woman's nudity, tormented me. My solitude was not pure. I was tormented, as ninety-nine per cent of our boys are. I was horrified, I was in agony, I prayed, and I fell. I was already depraved in imagination and in fact, but I had not yet taken the last step. I was perishing, but I hadn't yet laid hands on another human being. But one day a comrade of my brother's, a jolly student, a so-called good fellow, that is, the worst kind of good-for-nothing, who had taught us to drink and to play cards, persuaded us after a carousal to go *there*. We went. My brother was also still innocent, and he fell that same night. And I, a lad of fifteen, defiled myself and took part in defiling a woman, without in the least understanding what I was doing.

'I heard no word from any of my elders that what I was doing was wrong, you know. And indeed no one does hear it now. It is true it is in the Ten Commandments but then the Commandments are only needed to answer the priest at scripture examination, and even then they are not very necessary, not nearly as necessary as the commandment about the use of *ut* in conditional sentences in Latin.

'And so I never heard those older persons whose opinions I respected say that it was an evil. On the contrary, I heard people I respected say it was good. I had heard that my struggles and agonisings would be eased after that. I heard this and read it, and heard my elders say it would be good for my health, while from my comrades I heard that it was rather a fine, spirited thing to do. So in general I expected nothing but good from it. The risk of disease? But that too had been foreseen. A paternal government saw to that. It sees to the correct working of the brothels, and makes profligacy safe for schoolboys. Doctors too deal with it for a consideration. That is proper. They assert that debauchery is good for the health, and they organize proper well-regulated debauchery. I personally know mothers who take just such measures on behalf of their sons' health. And science sends them to the brothels.'

'Why do you say "science"?' I asked.

'Why, who are the doctors but the priests of science? Who deprave youths by maintaining that this is necessary for their health? They do.

'Yet if a one-hundredth part of the efforts devoted to the cure of syphilis were devoted to the eradication of debauchery there would long ago not have been a trace of syphilis left. As it is, efforts are made not to eradicate debauchery but to encourage it and to make debauchery safe. That is not the point, however. The point is that with me—and with nine-tenths, if not more, not of our class only but of all classes, even the peasants—this terrible thing happens that happened to me; I fell not because I succumbed to the natural temptation of a particular woman's charm—no, I was not seduced by a woman—but I fell because, in the set around me, what was really a fall was regarded by some as a most legitimate function good for one's health, and by others as a very natural and not only excusable but even innocent amusement for a young man. I did not have an inkling that it was a fall, but simply indulged in that half-pleasure, half-need, which, as was suggested to me, was natural at a certain age. I began to indulge in debauchery in the same way that I began to drink and to smoke. Yet in that first fall there was something special and pathetic. I remember that at once, then and there before I left the room, I felt sad, so sad that I wanted to cry—to cry for the loss of my innocence and for my relationship with women, now sullied for ever. Yes, my natural, simple relationship with women was spoilt for ever.

'From that time I have not had, and could not have, pure relations with women. I had become what is called a libertine. To be a libertine is a physical condition like that of a junkie, a drunkard, or a smoker. As a junkie, a drunkard, or a smoker is no longer normal, so too a man who has known several women for his pleasure is not normal but is a man perverted for ever, a libertine. As a drunkard or a junkie can be recognized at once by his face and manner, so too I became such a man. A libertine may restrain himself, may struggle, but he will never have those pure, simple, clear, brotherly relations with a woman. By the way he looks at a young woman and examines her, a voluptuary can always be recognized. I had become and I remained a voluptuary, and it was this that brought me to ruin.

V

'Ah, yes! After that things went from bad to worse, and there were all sorts of deviations. Oh, God! When I recall the abominations I committed in this respect I am seized with repulsion! And that is true of me, whom my companions, I remember, ridiculed for my so-called innocence. And when one hears of the "gilded youths" of officers, of the "Parisians" . . . ! And when all these gentlemen, and I—who have on our souls hundreds of the most varied and horrible crimes against women—when we thirty-year-old profligates, meticulously washed, shaved, perfumed, in clean linen and in evening dress or uniform, enter a drawing-room or ball-room, we are emblems of purity! Charming!

'Just think of what ought to be, and of what actually is! When in society such a gentleman comes up to my sister or daughter, I, knowing his life, ought to go up to him, take him aside, and say quietly, "My dear fellow, I know the life you lead, and how and with whom you pass your nights. This is no place for you. There are pure, innocent girls here. Be off!" That is what ought to be; but what happens is that when such a gentleman comes and dances, embracing our sister or daughter, we are jubilant, if he is rich and well-connected. Maybe after Rigulboche he will honour my daughter! Even if traces of disease remain, no matter! They are clever at curing that nowadays. Oh, yes, I know several girls in the best society whose parents enthusiastically gave them in marriage to men suffering from a certain disease. Oh, oh . . . the abomination of it! But a time will come when this abomination and falsehood will be exposed!'

He made his strange noise several times and again drank tea. It was fearfully strong and there was no water with which to dilute it. I felt much stimulated by the two glasses I had drunk. Probably the tea affected him too, for he became more and more animated. His voice grew increasingly mellow and expressive. He continually changed his position, now taking off his cap and now putting it on again, and his face changed strangely in the semi-darkness in which we were sitting.

'Well, so I lived till I was thirty, not abandoning for a moment the intention of marrying and arranging for myself a most elevated and pure family life. With that purpose I surveyed the scene for suitable girls,' he continued. 'I weltered in a mire of debauchery and at the same time was on the lookout for a girl pure enough to be worthy of me.'

'I rejected many just because they were not spotless enough to suit me, but at last I found one whom I considered worthy. She was one of two daughters of a once-wealthy Penza landowner who had been ruined.

'One evening after we had been out in a boat and had returned by moonlight, and I was sitting beside her admiring her curls and her shapely figure in a tight-fitting jersey, I suddenly decided that it was she! It seemed to me that evening that she understood all that I felt and thought, and that what I felt and thought was very lofty. In reality it was only that the jersey and the curls were particularly becoming and that after a day spent near her I wanted to be still closer.

'It is amazing how complete is the delusion that beauty is goodness. A handsome woman talks nonsense, you listen and hear not nonsense but cleverness. She says and does hateful things, and you see only charm. And if a handsome woman does not say stupid or hateful things, you at once persuade yourself that she is wonderfully clever and moral.

'I returned home in rapture, decided that she was the acme of moral perfection, and that therefore she was worthy to be my wife, and I proposed to her next day.

'What a muddle it is! Out of a thousand men who marry (not only among us but unfortunately also among the masses) there is hardly one who has not already been married ten, a hundred, or even, like Don Juan, a thousand times, before his wedding.

'It is true as I have heard and have myself observed that there are nowadays some chaste young men who feel and know that this thing is not a joke but an important matter.

'God help them! But in my time there was not one such in ten thousand. Everybody knows this and pretends not to. In all the novels they describe in detail the heroes' feelings and the ponds and bushes beside which they walk, but when their great love for some maiden is described, nothing is said about what has happened to these interesting heroes before: not a word about their frequenting certain houses, or about the servant-girls, cooks, and other people's wives! If there are such improper novels they are not put into the hands of those who most need this information—the unmarried girls.

'We first pretend to these girls that the profligacy which fills half the life of our towns, and even of the villages, does not exist at all. Then we get so accustomed to this pretence that at last, like the English, we ourselves really begin to believe that we are all moral people and live in a moral world. The girls, poor things, believe this quite seriously. So too did my unfortunate wife. I remember how, when we were engaged, I showed her my diary, from which she could learn something, if but a little, of my past, especially about my last *liaison* of which she might hear from others, and about which I therefore felt it necessary to inform her. I remember her horror, despair, and confusion, when she learnt of it and comprehend it. I saw then that she wanted to give me up. And why did she not do so? . . .'

He again made that sound, swallowed another mouthful of tea, and remained silent for a while.

VI

'No, after all, it's better like that, better ike that!' he exclaimed. 'It served me right! But that's not to the point—I meant to say that it's only the unfortunate girls who are deceived.

'The mothers know it, especially mothers educated by their own husbands—they know it very well. While pretending to believe in the purity of men, they act quite differently. They know with what sort of bait to catch men for themselves and for their daughters.

'You see it is only we men who don't know (because we don't wish to know) what women know very well, that the most exalted poetic love, as we call it, depends not on moral qualities but on physical nearness and on the *coiffure,* and the colour and cut of the dress. Ask an expert coquette who has set herself the task of captivating a man, which she would prefer to risk: to be convicted in his presence of lying, of cruelty, or even of dissoluteness, or to appear before him in an ugly and badly made dress—she will always opt for the first. She knows that we are continually lying about high sentiments, but really only want her body and will therefore forgive any abomination except an ugly tasteless costume that is in bad style.

'A coquette knows that consciously, and every innocent girl knows it unconsciously just as animals do.

'That is why there are those detestable jerseys, bustles, and naked shoulders, arms—all but breasts. A woman, especially if she has passed the male school, knows very well that all the talk about elevated subjects is just talk, but that what a man wants is her body and all that presents it in the most deceptive but alluring light; and she acts accordingly. If we only throw aside our familiarity with this indecency, which has become a second nature to us, and look at the life of our upper classes as it is, in all its shamelessness—why, it is simply a brothel . . . You don't agree? Allow me, I'll prove it,' he said, interrupting me. 'You say that the women of our society have other interests in life than prostitutes have, but I say no, and will prove it. If people differ in the aims of their lives, by the inner content of their lives, this difference will necessarily be reflected in externals and their externals will be different. But look at those unfortunate despised women and at the highest society ladies: the same costumes, the same fashions, the same perfumes, the exposure of arms, shoulders, and breasts, the same tight skirts over prominent bustles, the same passion for little stones, for costly, glittering objects, the same amusements, dances, music and singing. As those I first mentioned employ all means to allure, so do these other ladies.'

VII

'Well, just so these jerseys and curls and bustles caught me!

'It was very easy to catch me for I was brought up in the conditions in which amorous young people are forced like cucumbers in a greenhouse. Don't you see? Our stimulating superabundance of food, together with complete physical idleness, is nothing but a systematic excitement of desire. Whether this astonishes you or not, it is so. Why, till quite recently I didn't see anything of this myself, but now I have. That's why it torments me that nobody knows this, and people talk such nonsense as that lady did.

'Yes, last spring some peasants were working in our neighbourhood on a railway embankment. The usual food of a young peasant is rye-bread, kvas, and onions; he keeps alive and is vigorous and healthy; his work is light agricultural work. When he goes to railway-work his rations are buckwheat porridge and a pound of meat a day. But he works off that pound of meat during his sixteen hours' work wheeling barrow-loads of half-a-ton weight, so it is just enough for him. But we who every day consume two pounds of meat, and game, and fish and all sorts of heating foods and drinks—where does that go to? Into excesses of sensuality. And if it goes there and the safety-valve is open, all is well; but try and close the safety-valve, as I closed it temporarily, and at once a stimulus arises: passing through the prism of our artificial life, it expresses itself in utter infatuation. So I fell in love as they all do.

'Everything was there to hand: raptures, tenderness, and poetry. In reality that love of mine was the result, on the one hand of her mamma's and the dressmakers' activity, and on the other of the super-abundance of food consumed by me while living an idle life. If on the one hand there had been no boating, no dressmaker with her waists and so forth, and had my wife been sitting at home in a shapeless dressing-gown, and had I on the other hand been in circumstances normal to man—consuming just enough food to suffice for the work I did, and had the safety-valve been open—it happened to be closed at the time—I should not have fallen in love and nothing of all this would have happened.

VIII

'Well, it now so chanced that everything combined—my condition, her becoming dress, and the boating excursion. It had failed twenty times but now it succeeded. Just like a trap!

'I am not joking. You see nowadays marriages are arranged that way—like traps. What is the natural way? The lass is ripe, she must be given in marriage. It seems very simple if the girl is not a fright and there are men wanting to marry. That is how it was done in olden times. The wench became of age and her parents arranged the marriage. So it was done, and is done, among all mankind—Chinese, Hindus, Mohammedans, and among our own working classes; so it is done among at least ninety-nine per cent of the human race. Only among one per cent or less, among us voluptuaries, has it been discovered that that is not right, and something new has been invented. And what is this novelty? It is that the maidens sit around and the men walk about, as at a bazaar, choosing. And the maidens wait and think, but dare not say: "Me, please!" "No me!" "Not her, but me!" "Look what shoulders and other things I have!" And we men stroll around and look, and are very pleased. "Yes, I know! I won't be caught!" They stroll about and look, and are very pleased that everything is arranged like that for them. And then in an unguarded moment—snap! He is caught!'

'Then how ought it to be done?' I asked. 'Should the woman propose?'

'Oh, I don't know how; only if there's to be equality, let it be equality. If they have discovered that pre-arranged matches are degrading, why this is a thousand times worse! Then the rights and chances were equal, but here the woman is a slave in a bazaar or the bait in a trap. Tell any mother, or the girl herself, the truth, that she is only occupied in catching a husband... oh dear! what an insult! Yet they all do it and have nothing else to do. What is so terrible is to see sometimes quite innocent poor young girls engaged on it. And again, if it were but done openly—but it is always done deceitfully. "Ah, the Origin of Species, how interesting!" "Oh, Lily takes such an interest in painting! And will you be going to the exhibition? How instructive!" And the troika-drives, and shows, and symphonies! "Oh! how remarkable! My Lily is mad on music." "And why don't you share these convictions?" And boating... But their one thought is: "Take me, take me!" "Take my Lily!" "Or try—at least!" Oh, what an abomination! What falsehood!' he concluded, finishing his tea and beginning to put away the tea-things.

IX

'You know,' he went on while packing the tea and sugar into his bag. 'The domination by women from which the world suffers all arises from this.'

'What "domination by women"?' I asked. 'The rights, the legal privileges, are on the man's side.'

'Yes, yes! That's just it,' he interrupted me. 'That's just what I want to say. It explains the extraordinary phenomenon that on the one hand woman is reduced to the lowest level of humiliation, while on the other she dominates. Just like the Jews: as they pay us back for their oppression by a financial domination, so it is with women. "Ah, you want us to be traders only—all right, as traders we will dominate you!" say the Jews. "Ah, you want us to be merely objects of sensuality—all right, as objects of sensuality we will enslave you," say the women. Woman's lack of rights arises not from the fact that she must not vote or be a judge—to be occupied with such affairs is no privilege—but from the fact that she is not man's equal in sexual intercourse and has not the right to use a man or abstain from him as she likes—is not allowed to choose a man at her pleasure instead of being chosen by him. You say that is monstrous. Very well! Then a man must not have those rights either. As things are, a woman is deprived of that right while a man has it. And to make up for that right she acts on man's sensuality, and through his sensuality subdues him so that he only chooses formally, while in reality it is she who chooses. And once she has obtained these means she abuses them and acquires a terrible power over people.'

'But where is this special power?' I inquired.

'Where is it? Why everywhere, in everything! Go round the shops in any big town. There are goods worth millions and you cannot estimate the human labour expended on them, and look whether in nine-tenths of these shops there is anything for the use of men. All the luxuries of life are demanded and maintained by women.

'Count all the factories. An enormous proportion of them produce useless ornaments, carriages, furniture, and trinkets, for women. Millions of people, generations of slaves, perish at hard labour in factories merely to satisfy woman's caprice. Women, like queens, keep nine-tenths of mankind in bondage to heavy labour. And all because they have been abased and deprived of equal rights with men. And they revenge themselves by acting on our sensuality and catch us in their nets. Yes, it all comes of that.

'Women have made of themselves such an instrument for acting upon our sensuality that a man cannot quietly consort with a woman. As soon as a man approaches a woman he succumbs to her stupefying influence and becomes intoxicated and crazy. I used formerly to feel uncomfortable and uneasy when I saw a lady dressed up for a ball, but now I am simply frightened and plainly see her as something dangerous and illicit. I want to call a policeman and ask for protection from the peril, and demand that the dangerous object be removed and put away.

'Ah, you are laughing!' he exclaimed at me, 'but it is not at all a joke. I am sure a time will come, and perhaps very soon, when people will understand this and will wonder how a society could exist in which actions were permitted which so disturb social tranquillity as those adornments of the body directly evoking sensuality, which we tolerate for women in our society. Why, it's like setting all sorts of traps along the paths and promenades— it is even worse! Why is gambling forbidden while women in costumes which evoke sensuality are not forbidden? They are a thousand times more dangerous!'

X

'Well, you see, that was the way I was caught. I was what is called "in love". I not only imagined her to be the height of perfection, but during the time of our engagement I regarded myself also as the height of perfection. You know there is no rascal who cannot, if he tries, find rascals in some respects worse than himself, and who consequently cannot find reasons for pride and self-satisfaction. So it was with me: I was not marrying for money—covetousness had nothing to do with it—unlike the majority of my acquaintances who married for money or connections—I was rich, she was poor. That was one thing. Another thing I prided myself on was that while others married intending to continue in future the same polygamous life they had lived before marriage, I was firmly resolved to be monogamous after marriage, and there was no limit to my pride on that score. Yes, I was a dreadful pig and imagined myself to be an angel.

'Our engagement did not last long. I cannot now think of that time without shame! What nastiness! Love is supposed to be spiritual and not sensual. Well, if the love is spiritual, a spiritual communion, then that spiritual communion should find expression in words, in conversations, in discourse. There was nothing of the kind. It used to be dreadfully difficult to talk when we were left alone. It was the labour of Sisyphus. As soon as we thought of something to say and said it, we had again to be silent, devising something else. There was nothing to talk about. All that could be said about the life that awaited us, our arrangements and plans, had been said, and what was there more?

'Now if we had been animals we should have known that speech was unnecessary; but here on the contrary it was necessary to speak, and there was nothing to say, because we were not occupied with what finds vent in speech. And moreover there was that ridiculous custom of giving sweets, of coarse gourmandizing on sweets, and all those abominable preparations for the wedding: remarks about the house, the bedroom, beds, wraps, dressing-gowns, under-clothing, costumes. You must remember that if one married according to the injunctions of *Domostroy,* as that old fellow was saying, then the feather-beds, the trousseau, and the bedstead are all but details appropriate to the sacrament. But among us, when of ten who marry there are certainly nine who not only do not believe in the sacrament, but do not even believe that what they are doing entails certain obligations—where scarcely one man out of a hundred has not been married before, and of fifty scarcely one is not preparing in advance to be unfaithful to his wife at every convenient opportunity—when the majority regard the going to church as only a special condition for obtaining possession of a certain woman—think what a dreadful significance all these details acquire. They show the whole business to be only that; they show it to be a kind of sale. An innocent girl is sold to a profligate, and the sale is accompanied by certain formalities.

XI

'That is how everybody marries and that is how I married, and the much vaunted honeymoon began. What bothers me is the name itself.

'In Paris I once went to see the sights, and noticing a bearded woman and a water-dog on a sign-board, I entered the show. It turned out to be nothing but a man in a woman's low-necked dress, and a dog done up in walrus skin and swimming in a bath. It was very far from being interesting; but as I was leaving the showman politely saw me out and, addressing the public at the entrance, pointed to me and said, "Ask the gentleman whether it is not worth seeing! Come in, come in, one franc apiece!" I felt ashamed to say it was not worth seeing, and the showman had probably counted on that. It must be the same with those who have experienced the abomination of a honeymoon and who do not disillusion others. Neither did I disillusion anyone, but I do not now see why I should not tell the truth. Indeed, I think it needful to tell the truth about it. One felt awkward, ashamed, repelled, sorry, and above all dull, intolerably dull! It was something like what I felt when I learnt to smoke—when I felt sick and the saliva gathered in my mouth and I swallowed it and pretended that it was very pleasant. Pleasure from smoking, just as from that, if it comes at all, comes later. The husband must cultivate that vice in his wife in order to derive pleasure from it.'

'Why vice?' I said, 'You are speaking of the most natural human functions.'

'Natural?' he said. 'Natural? No, I may tell you that I have come to the conclusion that it is, on the contrary, *un*natural. Yes, quite *un*natural. Ask a child, ask an unperverted girl. Natural, you say!

'It is natural to eat. And to eat is, from the very beginning, enjoyable, easy, pleasant, and not shameful; but this is horrid, shameful, and painful. No, it is unnatural! And an unspoilt girl, as I have convinced myself, always hates it.'

'But how,' I asked, 'would the human race continue?'

'Yes, would not the human race perish?' he said, irritably and ironically, as if he had expected this familiar and insincere objection. 'Teach abstention from child-bearing so that English lords may always grow fat—that is all right. Preach it for the sake of greater pleasure—that is all right; but just hint at abstention from child-bearing in the name of morality—and, my goodness, what a rumpus . . . ! Isn't there a danger that the human race may die out because they want to cease to be swine?

'But forgive me! This light is unpleasant, may I shade it?' he said, pointing to the lamp.

'I said I did not mind; and with the haste with which he did everything, he got up on the seat and drew the woollen shade over the lamp.

'All the same,' I said, 'if everyone thought this the right thing to do, the human race would cease to exist.'

He did not reply at once.

'You ask how the human race will continue to exist,' he said, having again sat down in front of me, and spreading his legs far apart he leant his elbows on his knees. 'Why should it continue?'

'Why? If not, we should not exist.'

'And why should we exist?'

'Why? In order to live, of course.'

'But why live? If life has no aim, if life is given us for life's sake, there is no reason for living. And if it is so, then the Schopenhauers, the Hartmanns, and all the Buddhists as well, are quite right. But if life has an aim, it is clear that it ought to come to an end when that aim is reached. And so it turns out,' he said with noticeable agitation, evidently prizing his thought very highly. 'So it turns out. Just think: if the aim of humanity is goodness, righteousness, love—call it what you will—if it is what the prophets have said, that all mankind should be united together in love, that the spears should be beaten into pruning-hooks and so forth, what is it that hinders the attainment of this aim? The passions hinder it. Of all the passions the strongest, cruellest, and most stubborn is the sex-passion, physical love; and therefore if the passions are destroyed, including the strongest of them—physical love—the prophecies will be fulfilled, mankind will be brought into a unity, the aim of human existence will be attained, and there will be nothing further to live for.

'As long as mankind exists, the ideal is before it. And of course its ideal is not the rabbits' and pigs' ideal of breeding as fast as possible, nor that of monkeys or Parisians—to enjoy sex-passion in the most refined manner, but the ideal of goodness attained by continence and purity. Towards that people have always striven and still strive. You see what follows.

'It follows that physical love is a safety-valve. If the present generation has not attained its aim, it has not done so because of its passions, of which the sex-passion is the strongest. And if the sex-passion endures there will be a new generation and consequently the possibility of attaining the aim in the next generation. If the next one does not attain it, then the next after that may, and so on, till the aim is attained, the prophecies fulfilled, and mankind attains unity.

'But if not, what would result? If one admits that God created men for the attainment of a certain aim, and created them mortal but sexless, or created them immortal, what would be the result? Why, if they were mortal but without the sex-passion, and died without attaining the aim, God would have had to create new people to attain his aim. If they were immortal, let us grant that (though it would be more difficult for the same people to correct their mistakes and approach perfection than for those of another generation) they might attain that aim after many thousands of years, but then what use would they be afterwards? What could be done with them? It is best as it is. . . .

'But perhaps you don't like that way of putting it? Perhaps you are an evolutionist? It comes to the same thing. The highest race of animals, the human race, in order to maintain itself in the struggle with other animals ought to unite into one whole like a swarm of bees, and not breed continually; it should bring up sexless members as the bees do; that is, again, it should strive towards continence and not towards inflaming desire—to which the whole system of our life in now directed.'

He paused. 'The human race will cease? But can anyone doubt it, whatever his outlook on life may be? Why, it is as certain as death. According to all the teaching of the Church the end of the world will come, and according to all the teaching of science the same result is inevitable.'

He stopped, and stayed silent, drinking and smoking. Having smoked a cigarette to its butt, he took several more out of the bag and began packing them into his stained red cigarette-case.

'Something like that is taught by the Shakers,' I commented

'Yes, yes, they are right,' he exclaimed. 'Passion, no matter how it is glossed over, is an evil, a fearful evil, to be controlled, not encouraged as it is in our society. The words of the Gospel, "whosoever looketh upon a woman and lusteth after her, hath committed adultery in his heart," apply not merely to other men's wives but also, and specifically, to one's own. In the world as it is, the prevailing opinions are precisely contrary to this, and consequently to what they ought to be. What are the wedding trips and excursions and the seclusion of a young married couple as authorised by their elders, but licensed debauchery?'

XII

'But a moral law avenges itself when it is violated. Hard as I tried to make a success of my honeymoon, nothing came of it. It was horrid, shameful, and dull, the whole time. And very soon I began also to experience a painful, oppressive feeling. That began very quickly. I think it was on the third or fourth day that I found my wife depressed. I began asking her the reason and embracing her, which in my view was all she could want, but she removed my arm and began to cry. What about? She could not say. But she felt sad and distressed. Probably her exhausted nerves suggested to her the truth as to the vileness of our relation but she did not know how to express it.

'I began to question her, and she said something about feeling sad without her mother. It seemed to me that this was untrue, and I began comforting her without alluding to her mother. I did not understand that she was simply depressed and her mother was merely an excuse. But she immediately took offence because I had not mentioned her mother, as though I did not believe her. She told me she saw that I did not love her. I reproached her with being capricious, and suddenly her face changed entirely and instead of sadness it expressed irritation, and with the most venomous words she began accusing me of selfishness and cruelty.

'I gazed at her. Her whole face showed complete coldness and hostility, almost hatred. I remember how horror-struck I was when I saw this. "How? What?" I thought. "Love is a union of souls—and instead of that there is this! Impossible, this is not she!" I tried to soften her, but encountered such an insuperable wall of cold virulent hostility that before I had time to turn round I too was seized with irritation and we said a great many unpleasant things to one another. The impression of that first quarrel was dreadful. I call it a quarrel, but it was not a quarrel but only the disclosure of the abyss that really existed between us. Amorousness was exhausted by the satisfaction of sensuality and we were left confronting one another in our true relation: that is, as two egotists quite alien to each other who wished to get as much pleasure as possible each from the other. Indeed, it was not a quarrel, only the consequence of the cessation of sensuality revealing the reality of our relationship. I did not understand that this cold and hostile relation was our normal state: I did not understand it because at first this hostile attitude was very soon concealed from us by a renewal of redistilled sensuality, that is by love-making.

'I thought we had quarrelled and made it up again, and that it would not recur. But during that same first month of honeymoon a period of satiety soon returned, we again ceased to need one another, and another quarrel supervened. This second quarrel struck me even more painfully that the first. "So the first one was not an accident but was bound to happen and will happen again," I thought. I was all the more staggered by that second quarrel because it arose from such an impossible pretext. It had something to do with money, which I never grudged and could certainly not have grudged to my wife. I only remember that she gave the matter such a twist that some remark of mine appeared to be an expression of a desire on my part to dominate over her by means of money, to which I was supposed to assert an exclusive right—it was something impossibly stupid, mean, and not natural either to me or to her. I became exasperated, and upbraided her with lack of consideration for me. She accused me of the same thing, and it all began again. In her words and in the expression of her face and eyes I again noticed the cruel cold hostility that had so staggered me before. I had formerly quarrelled with my brother, my friends, and my father, but there had never, I remember, been the special venomous malice which there was here. But after a while this mutual hatred was screened by amorousness, that is sensuality, and I still consoled myself with the thought that these two quarrels had been mistakes and could be remedied. But then a third and a fourth quarrel followed and I realized that it was not accidental, but that is was bound to happen and would happen so, and I was horrified at the prospect before me. At the same time I was tormented by the terrible thought that I alone lived on such bad terms with my wife, so unlike what I had expected, whereas this did not happen between other married couples. I did not know then that it is our common fate, but that everybody imagines, just as I did, that it is their peculiar misfortune, and everyone conceals this exceptional and shameful misfortune not only from others but even from himself and does not acknowledge it to himself.

'It began during the first days and continued all the time, ever increasing and growing more obdurate. In the depths of my soul I felt from the first weeks that I was lost, that things had not turned out as I expected, that marriage was not only no happiness but a very heavy burden; yet like everybody else I did not wish to acknowledge this to myself (I should not have acknowledged it even now but for the end that followed) and I concealed it not only from others but from myself too.

'Now I am astonished that I failed to see my real position. It might have been seen from the fact that the quarrels began on pretexts it was impossible to remember when they were over. Our reason was not quick enough to *devise* sufficient excuses for the animosity that always existed between us. But more striking still was the insufficiency of the excuses for our reconciliations. Sometimes there were words, explanations, even tears, but sometimes . . . oh! it is disgusting even now to think of it—after the most cruel words to one another, came sudden silent glances, smiles, kisses, embraces. . . . Faugh, how horrid! How is it I did not then see all the vileness of it?'

XIII

Two new passengers entered and settled down on the farthest seats. He was silent while they were finding their places but as soon as they were properly seated continued, not for a moment losing the thread of his idea.

'You know, what is vilest about it,' he resumed, 'is that in theory love is something ideal and exalted, but in practice it is something abominable, swinish, which it is horrid and shameful to mention or remember. It is not for nothing that nature has made it disgusting and shameful. If it is disgusting and shameful one must understand that it is so. Yet here, quite contrarily, people pretend that what is disgusting and shameful is beautiful and lofty. What were the first symptoms of my love? Why, that I gave way to animal excesses, not only without shame but being somehow even proud of the possibility of these physical excesses, and without in the least considering either her spiritual or even her physical life. I wondered what embittered us, one with the other, yet it was perfectly simple: that animosity was nothing but the protest of our human nature against the animal nature that had overpowered it.

'I was surprised at our enmity to one another; yet it could not have been otherwise. That hatred was nothing but the mutual hatred of accomplices in a crime—both for the incitement to the crime and for the part taken in it. What was it but a crime when she, poor thing, became pregnant in the first month and our *swinish* connection continued? You think I am straying from my subject? Not at all! I am telling you *how* I killed my wife. They asked me at the trial with what and how I killed her. Fools! They thought I killed her with a knife, on the 5th of October. It was not then I killed her, but much earlier. Just as they are all now killing their wives, all, all. . . .'

'But how?' I asked.

'That's just what is so surprising, that nobody wants to see what is so manifestly obvious—what doctors ought to know and preach, but are silent about. Yet the matter is very simple. Men and women are created like the animals so that physical love is followed by pregnancy and then by suckling—conditions under which physical love is bad for the woman and for her child. There are an equal number of men and women. What follows from this? It seems clear enough: no great wisdom is needed to draw the conclusion that animals do, namely, the need of continence. But no such conclusion is drawn. Science goes on to discover some kind of organisms that run about in the blood, and all sorts of useless nonsense, but cannot grasp the point. At least one doesn't hear of science teaching it!

'And so a woman has only two ways out: one is to make a monster of herself, to destroy and go on destroying within herself to such degree as may be necessary the capacity of being a woman, that is, a mother, in order that a man may quietly and continuously get his enjoyment; the other way out—and it's not even a way out but a simple, coarse, and direct violation of the laws of nature (practised in all so-called decent families) is that, contrary to her nature, the woman must be her husband's mistress even while she is pregnant or nursing—must be what not even an animal descends to, and for which her strength is insufficient. That is what provokes nervous problems and hysteria in our class, and among the peasants causes what they call being "possessed by the devil"—epilepsy. You will notice that no pure maidens are ever "possessed", but only married women living with their husbands. That is so here, and it's just the same in Europe. All the hospitals for hysterical women are full of those who have violated nature's law. The epileptics and Charcot's patients are complete wrecks, you know, but the world is full of half-crippled women. Just think of it, what a great work goes on within a woman when she conceives or when she is nursing an infant. That which is growing will replicate us and replace us. And this sacred work is violated—by what? It is terrible to think of it! And they prate about the freedom and the rights of women!

It is as if cannibals fattened their captives to be eaten, and at the same time declared that they were concerned about their prisoners' rights and freedom.'

All this was new to me and startled me.

'What is one to do? If that is so,' I said, 'it means that one may love one's wife once in two years, yet men . . .'

'Men must!' he interrupted me. 'It's again those precious priests of science who have persuaded everybody of that. Imbue a man with the idea that he requires vodka, tobacco, or opium, and all these things will be indispensable to him. It seems that God didn't understand what was necessary and therefore, omitting to consult those wizards, arranged things badly. You see matters don't add up. They have decided that it's essential for a man to satisfy his desires, and the bearing and nursing of children comes and interferes with it and hinders the satisfaction of that need. What is one to do then? Consult the wizards! They will arrange it. And they have devised something. Oh! when will those wizards with their deceptions be dethroned? It is high time! It has come to such a point that people go mad and shoot themselves and all because of this. How could it be otherwise? The animals seem to know that their progeny continue their race, and they keep to a certain law in this matter. Man alone neither knows it nor wishes to know, but is concerned only to get all the pleasure he can. And who is doing that? The lord of nature—man! Animals, you see, only come together at times when they are capable of producing progeny, but the filthy lord of nature is at it any time if only it pleases him! And as if that were not sufficient, he exalts this apish occupation into the most precious pearl of creation, into love. In the name of this love, that is, this filth, he destroys—what? Why, half the human race! All the women who might help the progress of mankind towards truth and goodness he converts, for the sake of his pleasure, into enemies instead of helpmates. See what it is that everywhere impedes the forward movement of mankind. Women! And why are they what they are? For the reason just given.

'Yes, yes . . .' he repeated several times, and began to move about, and to get out his cigarettes and to smoke, evidently trying to calm himself.

XIV

'I too lived like a pig of that sort,' he continued in his former tone. 'The worst thing about it was that while living that horrid life I imagined that, because I did not go after other women, I was living an honest family life, that I was a moral man and in no way blameworthy, and if quarrels occurred it was her fault and resulted from her character.

'Of course the fault was not hers. She was like everybody else—like the majority of women. She had been brought up as the position of women in our society requires, and as therefore all women of the leisured classes without exception are brought up and cannot help being brought up. People talk about some new kind of education for women. It is all empty words: their education is exactly what it has to be in view of our unfeigned, real, general opinion about women.

'The education of women will always correspond to men's opinion about them. Don't we know how men regard women: Wine, Women and Song, and what the poets say in their verses! Take all poetry, all pictures and sculpture, beginning with love poems and the nude Venuses and Phrynes, and you will see that woman is an instrument of enjoyment; she is so on the Truba and the Grachevka, and also at the Court balls. And note the devil's cunning: if they are here for enjoyment and pleasure, let it be known that it is pleasure and that woman is a sweet morsel. But no, first the knights-errant declare that they worship women (worship her, and yet regard her as an instrument of enjoyment), and now people assure us that they respect women. Some give up their places to her, pick up her handkerchief;

others acknowledge her right to occupy all positions and to take part in the government, and so on. They do all that, but their outlook on her remains the same. She is a means of enjoyment. Her body is a means of enjoyment. And she knows this.

'It is just as it is with slavery. Slavery, you know, is nothing else than the exploitation by some of the unwilling labour of many. Therefore to get rid of slavery it is necessary that people should not wish to profit by the forced labour of others and should consider it a sin and a shame. But they go and abolish the external form of slavery and arrange things so that one can no longer buy and sell slaves, and they imagine and assure themselves that slavery no longer exists, and do not see or wish to see that it does, because people still want and consider it good and right to exploit the labour of others. And as long as they consider that good, there will always be people stronger or more cunning than others who will succeed in doing it. So it is with the emancipation of woman: the enslavement of woman lies simply in the fact that people desire, and think it good, to avail themselves of her as a tool of enjoyment. Well, and they liberate woman, give her all sorts of rights equal to man, but continue to regard her as an instrument of enjoyment, and so educate her in childhood and afterwards by public opinion. And there she is, still the same humiliated and depraved slave, and the man still a depraved slave-owner.

'They emancipate women in universities and in law courts, but continue to regard her as an object of enjoyment. Teach her, as she is taught among us, to regard herself as such, and she will always remain an inferior being. Either with the help of those scoundrels the doctors she will prevent the conception of offspring—that is, will be a complete prostitute, lowering herself not to the level of an animal but to the level of a thing—or she will be what the majority of women are, mentally diseased, hysterical, unhappy, and lacking capacity for spiritual development. High schools and universities cannot alter that. It can only be changed by a change in men's outlook on women and women's way of regarding themselves. It will change only when woman regards virginity as the highest state, and does not, as at present, consider the highest state of a human being a shame and a disgrace. While that is not so, the ideal of every girl, whatever her education may be, will continue to be to attract as many men as possible, as many males as possible, so as to have the possibility of choosing.

'But the fact that one of them knows more mathematics, and another can play the harp, makes no difference. A woman is happy and attains all she can desire when she has bewitched a man. Therefore the chief aim of a woman is to be able to bewitch him. So it has been and will be. So it is in her maiden life in our society, and so it continues to be in her married life. For a maiden this is necessary in order to have a choice, for the married woman in order to have power over her husband.

'The one thing that stops this or at any rate suppresses it for a time, is children, and then only if the mother is not a monster, that is, if she nurses them herself. But here the doctors again come in.

'My wife, who wanted to suckle, and did suckle the four later children herself, happened to be unwell after the birth of her first child. And those doctors, who cynically undressed her and felt her all over—for which I had to thank them and pay them money—those dear doctors considered that she must not suckle the child; and that first time she was deprived of the only means which might have kept her from coquetry. We engaged a wet nurse, that is, we took advantage of the poverty, the need, and the ignorance of a woman, tempted her away from her own baby to ours, and in return gave her a fine head-dress with gold lace. But that is not the point. The point is that during that time when my wife was free from pregnancy and from suckling, the feminine coquetry which had lain dormant within her manifested itself with particular force. And coinciding with this the torments of jealousy rose up in me with a special force. They tortured me all my married life, as they cannot but torture all husbands who live with their wives as I did with mine, that is, immorally.

XV

'During the whole of my married life I never ceased to be tormented by jealousy, but there were periods when I specially suffered from it. One of these periods was when, after the birth of our first child, the doctors forbade my wife to suckle it. I was particularly jealous at that time, in the first place because my wife was experiencing that unrest natural to a mother which is sure to be aroused when the natural course of life is needlessly violated; and secondly, because seeing how easily she abandoned her moral obligations as a mother, I rightly though unconsciously concluded that it would be equally easy for her to disregard her duty as a wife, especially as she was quite well and in spite of the precious doctors' prohibition was able to suckle her later children admirably.'

'I see you don't like doctors,' I said, noticing a peculiarly malevolent tone in his voice whenever he alluded to them.

'It is not a case of liking or disliking. They have ruined my life as they have ruined and are ruining the lives of thousands and hundreds of thousands of human beings, and I cannot help connecting the effect with the cause. I understand that they want to earn money like lawyers and others, and I would willingly give them half my income, and all who realize what they are doing would willingly give them half of their possessions, if only they would not interfere with our family life and would never come near us. I have not collected evidence, but I know dozens of cases (there are any number of them!) where they have killed a child in its mother's womb asserting that she could not give it birth, though she has had children quite safely later on; or they have killed the mother on the pretext of performing some operation. No one reckons these murders any more than they reckoned the murders of the Inquisition, because it is supposed that it is done for the good of mankind. It is impossible to number all the crimes they commit. But, all those crimes are as nothing compared to the moral corruption of materialism they introduce into the world, especially through women.

'I don't lay stress on the fact that if one is to follow their instructions, then on account of the infection which exists everywhere and in everything, people would not progress towards greater unity but towards separation; for according to their teaching we ought all to sit apart and not remove the carbolic atomizer from our mouths (though now they have discovered that even that is of no avail). But that does not matter either. The principal poison lies in the demoralization of the world, especially of women.

'Today one can no longer say: "You are not living rightly, live better." One can't say that, either to oneself or to anyone else. If you live a bad life it is caused by the abnormal functioning of your nerves and so on. So you must go to them, and they will prescribe eight penn'orth of medicine from a chemist, which you must take!

'You get still worse: then more medicine and the doctor again. An excellent trick!

'That however is not the point. All I wish to say is that she suckled her babies perfectly well and that only her pregnancy and the nursing of her babies saved me from the torments of jealousy. Had it not been for that it would all have happened sooner. The children saved me and her. In eight years she had five children and suckled all except the first herself.'

'And where are your children now?' I asked.

'The children?' he repeated in a frightened voice.

'Forgive me, perhaps it is painful for you to be reminded of them.'

'No, it does not matter. My wife's sister and brother have taken them. They would not let me have them. I gave them my estate, but they did not give them up to me. You know I am a sort of lunatic. I have left them now and am going away. I have seen them, but they won't let me have them because I might bring them up so that they would not be like their parents, and they have to be just like them. Oh well, what is to be done? Of course they won't let me have them and won't trust me. Besides, I do not know whether I should be able to bring them up. I think not. I am a ruin, a cripple. Still I have one thing in me. I know! Yes, that is true, I know what others are far from knowing.

'Yes, my children are living and growing up just such savages as everybody around them. I saw them, saw them three times. I can do nothing for them, nothing. I am now going to my place in the south. I have a little house and a small garden there.

'Yes, it will be a long time before people learn what I know. How much of iron and other metal there is in the sun and the stars is easy to find out, but anything that exposes our swinishness is difficult, terribly difficult!

'You at least listen to me, and I am grateful for that.

XVI

'You mentioned my children. There again, what terrible lies are told about children! Children a blessing from God, a joy! That's all a lie. It was so once upon a time, but now it is not so at all. Children are a torment and nothing else. Most mothers feel this quite plainly, and sometimes inadvertently say so. Ask most mothers of our propertied classes and they will tell you that they do not want to have children for fear of their falling ill and dying. They don't want to nurse them if they do have them, for fear of becoming too much attached to them and having to suffer. The pleasure a baby gives them by its loveliness, its little hands and feet, and its whole body, is not as great as the suffering caused by the very fear of its possibly falling ill and dying, not to speak of its actual illness or death. After weighing the advantages and disadvantages it seems disadvantageous, and therefore undesirable, to have children. They say this quite frankly and boldly, imagining that these feelings of theirs arise from their love of children, a good and laudable feeling of which they are proud. They do not notice that by this reflection they plainly repudiate love, and only affirm their own selfishness. They get less pleasure from a baby's loveliness than suffering from fear on its account, and therefore the baby they would love is not wanted. They do not sacrifice themselves for a beloved being, but sacrifice a being whom they might love, for their own sakes.

'It's clear that this is not love but selfishness. But one hasn't the heart to blame them—the mothers in well-to-do families—for that selfishness, when one remembers how dreadfully they suffer on account of their children's health, again thanks to the influence of those same doctors among our well-to-do classes. Even now, when I do but remember my wife's life and the condition she was in during the first years when we had three or four children and she was absorbed in them, I am seized with horror! We led no life at all, but were in a state of constant danger, of escape from it, recurring danger, again followed by a desperate struggle and another escape—always as if we were on a sinking ship. Sometimes it seemed to me that this was done on purpose and that she pretended to be anxious about the children in order to subdue me. It solved all questions in her favour with such tempting simplicity. It sometimes seemed as if all she did and said on these occasions was pretence. But no! She herself suffered terribly, and continually tormented herself about the children and their health and illnesses. It was torture for her and for me too; and it was impossible for her not to suffer. After all, the attachment to her children, the animal need of feeding, caressing, and protecting them, was there as with most women, but there was not the lack of imagination and reason that there is in animals. A hen is not afraid of what may happen to her chick, does not know all the diseases that may befall it, and does not know all those remedies with which people imagine that they can save from illness and death. And for a hen her young are not a source of torment. She does for them what it is natural and pleasurable for her to do; her young ones are a pleasure to her. When a chick falls ill her duties are quite definite: she warms and feeds it. And doing this she knows that she is doing all that is necessary. If her chick dies she does not ask herself why it died, or where it has gone to; she cackles for a while, and then leaves off and goes on living as before. But for our unfortunate women, my wife among them, it was not so. Not to mention illnesses and how to cure them, she was always hearing and reading from all sides endless rules for the rearing and educating of children, which were continually being superseded by others. This is the way to feed a child: feed it in this way, on such a thing; no, not on such a thing, but in this way; clothes, drinks, baths, putting to bed, walking, fresh air,—for all these things we, especially she, heard of new rules every week, just as if children had only begun to be born into the world since yesterday. And if a child that had not been fed or bathed in the right way or at the right time fell ill, it appeared that we were to blame for not having done what we ought.

'That was so while they were well. It was a torment even then. But if one of them happened to fall ill, it was all up: a regular hell! It's supposed that illness can be cured and that there is a science about it, and people—doctors—who know about it. Ah, but not all of them know—only the very best. When a child is ill one must get hold of the very best one, the one who saves, and then the child is saved; but if you don't get that doctor, or if you don't live in the place where that doctor lives, the child is lost. This was not a creed peculiar to her, it is the creed of all the women of our class, and she heard nothing else from all sides. Catherine Semenovna lost two children because Ivan Zakharych was not called in in time, but Ivan Zakharych saved Mary Ivanovna's eldest girl, and the Petrovs moved in time to various hotels by the doctor's advice, and the children remained alive; but if they had not been segregated the children would have died. Another who had a delicate child moved south by the doctor's advice and saved the child. How can she help being tortured and agitated all the time, when the lives of the children for whom she has an animal attachment depend on her finding out in time what Ivan Zakharych will say! But what Ivan Zakharych will say nobody knows, and he himself least of all, for he is well aware that he knows nothing and therefore cannot be of any use, but just shuffles about at random so that people should not cease to believe that he knows something or other. You see, had she been wholly an animal she would not have suffered so, and if she had been quite a human being she would have had faith in God and would have said and thought, as a believer does: "The Lord gave and the Lord hath taken away. One can't escape from God."

'Our whole life with the children, for my wife and consequently for me, was not a joy but a torment. How could she help torturing herself? She tortured herself incessantly. Sometimes when we had just made peace after some scene of jealousy, or simply after a quarrel, and thought we should be able to live, to read, and to think a little, we had no sooner settled down to some occupation than the news came that Vasya was being sick, or Masha showed symptoms of dysentery, or Andrusha had a rash, and there was an end to peace, it was not life any more. Where was one to drive to? For what doctor? How isolate the child? And then it's a case of enemas, temperatures, medicines, and doctors. Hardly is that over before something else begins. We had no regular settled family life but only, as I have already said, continual escapes from imaginary and real dangers. It is like that in most families nowadays, you know, but in my family it was especially acute. My wife was a child-loving and a credulous woman.

'So the presence of children not only failed to improve our life but poisoned it. Besides, the children were a new cause of dissension. As soon as we had children they became the means and the object of our discord, and more often the older they grew. They were not only the object of discord but the weapons of our strife. We used our children, as it were, to fight one another with. Each of us had a favourite weapon among them for our strife. I used to fight her chiefly through Vasya, the eldest boy, and she me through Lisa. Besides that, as they grew older and their characters became defined, it came about that they grew into allies whom each of us tried to draw to his or her side. They, poor things, suffered terribly from this, but we, with our incessant warfare, had no time to think of that. The girl was my ally, and the eldest boy, who resembled his mother and was her favourite, was often hateful to me.

XVII

'Well, and so we lived. Our relations to one another grew more and more hostile and at last reached a stage where it was not disagreement that caused hostility but hostility that caused disagreement. Whatever she might say I disagreed with beforehand, and it was just the same with her.

'In the fourth year we both, it seemed, came to the conclusion that we could not understand one another. We no longer tried to bring any dispute to a conclusion. We invariably kept to our own opinions even about the most trivial questions, but especially about the children. As I now recall them the views I maintained were not at all so dear to me that I could not have given them up; but she was of the opposite opinion and to yield meant yielding to her, and that I could not do. It was the same with her. She probably considered herself quite in the right towards me, and as for me I always thought myself a saint towards her. When we were alone together we were doomed almost to silence, or to conversations such as I am convinced animals can carry on with one another: "What's the time? Time to go to bed. What's for dinner today? Where shall we go? What's in the papers? Send for the doctor; Masha has a sore throat." We only needed to go a hairbreadth beyond this impossibly limited circle of conversation for irritation to flare up.

'We had collisions and acrimonious words about the coffee, a tablecloth, a trap, a lead at bridge, all of them things that could not be of any importance to either of us. In me at any rate there often raged a terrible hatred of her. Sometimes I watched her pouring out tea, swinging her leg, lifting a spoon to her mouth, smacking her lips and drawing in some liquid, and I hated her for these things as though they were the worst possible actions. I did not then notice that the periods of anger corresponded quite regularly and exactly to the periods of what we called love. A period of love—then a period of animosity; an energetic period of love, then a long period of animosity; a weaker manifestation of love, and a shorter period of animosity. We did not then understand that this love and animosity were one and the same animal feeling only at opposite poles. To live like that would have been awful had we understood our position; but we neither understood nor saw it. Both salvation and punishment for man lie in the fact that if he lives wrongly he can befog himself so as not to see the misery of his position. And this we did. She tried to forget herself in intense and always hurried occupation with household affairs, busying herself with the arrangements of the house, her own and the children's clothes, their lessons, and their health; while I had my own occupations: wine, my office duties, shooting, and cards. We were both continually occupied, and we both felt that the busier we were the nastier we might be to each other. "It's all very well for you to grimace," I thought, "but you have harassed me all night with your scenes, and I have a meeting on." "It's all very well for you," she not only thought but said, "but I have been awake all night with the baby." Those new theories of hypnotism, psychic diseases, and hysterics are not a simple folly, but a dangerous and repulsive one. Charcot would certainly have said that my wife was hysterical, and that I was abnormal, and he would no doubt have tried to cure me. But there was nothing to cure.

'Thus we lived in a perpetual fog, not seeing the condition we were in. And if what did happen had not happened, I should have gone on living so to old age and should have thought, when dying, that I had led a good life. I should not have realized the abyss of misery and the horrible falsehood in which I wallowed.

'We were like two convicts hating each other and chained together, poisoning one another's lives and trying not to see it. I did not then know that ninety-nine per cent of married people live in a similar hell to the one I was in and that it cannot be otherwise. I did not then know this either about others or about myself.

'It's strange what coincidences there are in regular, or even in irregular, lives! Just when the parents find life together unendurable, it becomes necessary to move to town for the children's education.'

He stopped, and once or twice gave vent to his strange sounds, which were now quite like suppressed sobs. We were approaching a station.

'What's the time?' he asked.

I looked at my watch. It was two o'clock.

'You aren't tired?' he asked.

'No, but you are?'

'I am suffocating. Excuse me, I will walk up and down and drink some water.'

He went unsteadily through the carriage. I remained alone thinking over what he had said, and I was so engrossed in thought that I did not notice when he reentered by the door at the other end of the carriage.

XVIII

'Yes, I keep diverging,' he began. 'I have thought much over it. I now see many things differently and I want to speak of it.

'Well, so we lived in town. In town a man can live for a hundred years without noticing that he has long been dead and has rotted away. He has no time to take account of himself, he is always occupied. Business affairs, social intercourse, health, art, the children's health and their education. Now one has to receive so-and-so and so-and-so, go to see so-and-so and so-and-so; now one has to go and look at this, and hear this man or that woman. In town, you know, there are at any given moment one or two, or even three, celebrities whom one must on no account miss seeing. Then one has to undergo a treatment oneself or get someone else attended to, then there are teachers, tutors, and governesses, but one's own life is quite empty. Well, so we lived and felt less the painfulness of living together. Besides at first we had splendid occupations, arranging things in a new place, in new quarters; and we were also occupied in going from the town to the country and back to town again.

'We lived so through one winter, and the next there occurred, unnoticed by anyone, an apparently unimportant thing, but the cause of all that happened later.

'She was not well and the doctors told her not to have children, and taught her how to avoid it. To me it was disgusting. I struggled against it, but she with frivolous obstinacy insisted on having her own way and I submitted. The last excuse for our swinish life—children—was then taken away, and life became viler than ever.

'To a peasant, a labouring man, children are necessary; though it is hard for him to feed them, still he needs them, and therefore his marital relations have a justification. But to us who have children, more children are unnecessary; they are an additional care and expense, a further division of property, and a burden. So our swinish life has no justification. We either artificially deprive ourselves of children or regard them as a misfortune, the consequences of carelessness, and that is still worse.

'We have no justification. But we've fallen morally so low that we do not even feel the need of any justification.

'The majority of the present educated world devote themselves to this kind of debauchery without the least qualm of conscience.

'There is indeed nothing that can feel qualms, for conscience in our society is non-existent, unless one can call public opinion and the criminal law a "conscience." In this case neither the one nor the other is infringed: there is no reason to be ashamed of public opinion for everybody acts in the same way—Mary Pavlovna, Ivan Zakharych, and the rest. Why breed paupers or deprive one-self of the possibility of social life? There's no need to fear or be ashamed in face of the criminal law either. Those shameless hussies, or soldiers' wives, throw their babies into ponds or wells, and they of course must be put into prison, but we do it all at the proper time and in a clean way.

'We lived like that for another two years. The means employed by those scoundrel-doctors evidently began to bear fruit; she became physically stouter and handsomer, like the late beauty of summer's end. She felt this and paid attention to her appearance. She developed a provocative kind of beauty which made people restless. She was in the full vigour of a well-fed and aroused woman of thirty who is not bearing children. Her appearance disturbed people. When she passed men she attracted their notice. She was like a fresh, well-fed, harnessed horse, whose bridle has been removed. There was no bridle, as is the case with ninety-nine hundredths of our women. And I felt this—and was frightened.'

XIX

He suddenly rose and sat down close to the window.

'Pardon me,' he muttered and, with his eyes fixed on the window, he remained silent for about three minutes. Then he sighed deeply and moved back to the seat opposite mine. His face was quite changed, his eyes looked pathetic, and his lips puckered strangely, almost as if he were smiling. 'I'm rather tired but I'll go on with it. We have still plenty of time, it is not dawn yet. Ah, yes,' he began after lighting a cigarette, 'she grew plumper after she stopped having babies, and her malady—that everlasting worry about the children—began to pass . . . at least not actually to pass, but she as it were woke up from an intoxication, came to herself, and saw that there was a whole divine world with its joys which she had forgotten, but a divine world she did not know how to live in and did not at all understand. "I must not miss it! Time is passing and won't come back!" So, I imagine, she thought, or rather felt, nor could she have thought or felt differently: she had been brought up in the belief that there was only one thing in the world worthy of attention—love. She had married and received something of that love, but not nearly what had been promised and was expected. Even that had been accompanied by many disappointments and sufferings, and then this unexpected torment: so many children! The torments exhausted her. And then, thanks to the obliging doctors, she learnt that it is possible to avoid having children. She was very glad, tried it, and became alive again for the one thing she knew—for love. But love with a husband, befouled by jealousy and all kinds of anger, was no longer the thing she wanted. She had visions of some other, clean, new love; at least I thought she had. And she began to look about her as if expecting something. I saw this and could not help feeling anxious. It happened again and again that while talking to me, as usual through other people—that is, telling a third person what she meant for me—she boldly, without remembering that she had expressed the opposite opinion an hour before, declared, though half-jokingly, that a mother's cares are a fraud, and that it is not worth while to devote one's life to children when one is young and can enjoy life. She gave less attention to the children, and less frenziedly than before, but gave more and more attention to herself, to her appearance (though she tried to conceal this), and to her pleasures, even to her accomplishments. She again enthusiastically took to the piano which she had quite abandoned, and it all began from that.'

He turned his weary eyes to the window again but, evidently making an effort, immediately continued once more.

'Yes, that man made his appearance . . .' he became confused and once or twice made that peculiar sound with his nose.

I could see that it was painful for him to name that man, to recall him, or speak about him. But he made an effort and, as if he had broken the obstacle that hindered him, continued resolutely.

'He was a worthless man in my opinion and according to my estimate. And not because of the significance he acquired in my life but because he really was so. However, the fact that he was a poor sort of fellow only served to show how irresponsible she was. If it had not been he then it would have been another. It had to be!'

Again he paused. 'Yes, he was a musician, a violinist; not a professional, but a semi-professional semi-society man.

'His father, a landowner, was a neighbour of my father's. He had been ruined, and his children—there were three boys—had obtained settled positions; only this one, the youngest, had been handed over to his godmother in Paris. There he was sent to the *Conservatoire* because he had a talent for music, and he came out as a violinist and played at concerts. He was a man . . .' Having evidently intended to say something bad about him, Pozdnyshev restrained himself and rapidly said: 'Well, I don't really know how he lived, I only know that he returned to Russia that year and appeared in my house.

'With moist almond-shaped eyes, red smiling lips, a small waxed moustache, hair done in the latest fashion, and an insipidly pretty face, he was what women call "not bad looking". His figure was weak though not misshapen, and he had a specially developed posterior, like a woman's, or such as Hottentots are said to have. They too are reported to be musical. Pushing himself as far as possible into familiarity, but sensitive and always ready to yield at the slightest resistance, he maintained his dignity in externals, wore buttoned boots of a special Parisian fashion, bright-coloured ties, and other things foreigners acquire in Paris, which by their noticeable novelty always attract women. There was an affected external gaiety in his manner. That manner, you know, of speaking about everything in allusions and unfinished sentences, as if you knew it all, remembered it, and could complete it yourself.

'It was he with his music who was the cause of it all. You know at the trial the case was put as if it was all caused by jealousy. No such thing; that is, I don't mean "no such thing", it was and yet it was not. At the trial it was decided that I was a wronged husband and that I had killed her while defending my outraged honour (that is the phrase they employ, you know). That is why I was acquitted. I tried to explain matters at the trial but they took it that I was trying to rehabilitate my wife's honour.

'What my wife's relations with that musician may have been has no meaning for me, or for her either. What has a meaning is what I have told you about—my swinishness. The whole thing was an outcome of the terrible abyss between us of which I have told you—that dreadful tension of mutual hatred which made the first excuse sufficient to produce a crisis. The quarrels between us had for some time past become frightful, and were all the more shaking because they alternated with similarly intense animal passion.

'If he had not appeared there would have been someone else. If the occasion had not been jealousy it would have been something else. I maintain that all husbands who live as I did, must either live dissolutely, separate, or kill themselves or their wives as I have done. If there is anybody who has not done so, he is a rare exception. Before I ended as I did, I had several times been on the verge of suicide, and she too had repeatedly tried to poison herself.

XX

'Well, that's how things were going not long before it happened. We seemed to be living in a state of truce and had no reason to infringe it. Then we chanced to speak about a dog which I said had been awarded a medal at an exhibition. She remarked, "Not a medal, but an honourable mention." A dispute ensues. We jump from one subject to another, reproach one another, "Oh, that's nothing new, it's always been like that." "You said . . ." "No, I didn't say so." "Then I am telling lies! . . ." You feel that at any moment that dreadful quarrelling which makes you wish to kill yourself or her will begin. You know it will begin immediately, and fear it like fire and therefore wish to restrain yourself, but your whole being is seized with fury. She being in the same or even a worse condition purposely misinterprets every word you say, giving it a wrong meaning. Her every word is venomous; where she alone knows that I am most sensitive, she stabs. It gets worse and worse. I shout: "Be quiet!" or something of that kind.

'She rushes out of the room and into the nursery. I try to hold her back in order to finish what I was saying, to prove my point, and I seize her by the arm. She pretends that I have hurt her and screams: "Children, your father is hitting me!" I shout: "Don't lie!" "But it's not the first time!" she screams, or something like that. The children rush to her. She calms them down. I say, "Don't sham!" She says, "Everything is sham in your eyes, you would kill any one and say they were shamming. Now I've understood you. That's just what you want!" "Oh, I wish you were dead as a dog!" I shout. I remember how those dreadful words horrified me. I never thought I could utter such dreadful, coarse words, and am surprised that they escaped me. I shout them and rush away into my study and sit down and smoke. I hear her go out into the hall preparing to go away. I ask, "Where are you going to?" She doesn't reply. "Well, devil take her," I say to myself, and go back to my study and lie down and smoke. A thousand different plans of how to revenge myself on her and get rid of her, and how to improve matters and go on as if nothing had happened, come into my head. I think all that and go on smoking and smoking. I think of running away from her, hiding myself, going to America. I get as far as dreaming of how I shall get rid of her, how splendid that will be, and how I shall unite with another, an admirable woman—quite different. I shall get rid of her either by her dying or by a divorce, and I plan how it is to be done. I notice that I am getting confused and not thinking of what is necessary, and to prevent myself from perceiving that my thoughts are not to the point I go on smoking.

'Life in the house goes on. The governess comes in and asks: "Where is madame? When will she be back?" The footman asks whether he is to serve tea. I go to the dining-room. The children, especially Lisa who already understands, gaze inquiringly and disapprovingly at me. We drink tea in silence. She has still not come back. The evening passes, she has not returned, and two different feelings alternate within me. Anger because she torments me and all the children by her absence which will end by her returning; and fear that she will not return but will do something to herself. I would go to fetch her, but where am I to look for her? At her sister's? But it would be so stupid to go and ask. And it's all the better: if she is bent on tormenting someone, let her torment herself. Besides, that is what she's waiting for; and next time it would be worse still. But suppose she is not with her sister but is doing something to herself, or has already done it! It's past ten, past eleven! I don't go to the bedroom—it would be stupid to lie there alone waiting—but I'll not lie down here either. I wish to occupy my mind, to write a letter or to read, but I can't do anything. I sit alone in my study, tortured, angry, and listening. It's three o'clock, four o'clock, and she is not back. Towards morning I fall asleep. I wake up, she has still not come!

'Everything in the house goes on in the usual way, but all are perplexed and look at me inquiringly and reproachfully, considering me to be the cause of it all. And in me the same struggle still continues: anger that she is torturing me, and anxiety for her.

'At about eleven in the morning her sister arrives as her envoy. And the usual talk begins. "She is in a terrible state. What does it all mean?" "After all, nothing has happened." I speak of her impossible character and say that I haven't done anything.

' "But, you know, it can't go on like this," says her sister.

' "It's all her doing and not mine," I say. "I won't take the first step. If it means separation, let it be separation."

'My sister-in-law goes away having achieved nothing. I had boldly said that I would not take the first step; but after her departure, when I came out of my study and saw the children piteous and frightened, I was prepared to take the first step. I should be glad to do it, but I don't know how. Again I pace up and down and smoke; at lunch I drink vodka and wine and attain what I unconsciously desire—I no longer see the stupidity and humiliation of my position.

'At about three she comes. When she meets me she does not speak. I imagine that she has submitted, and begin to say that I had been provoked by her reproaches. She, with the same stern expression on her terribly harassed face, says that she has not come for explanations but to fetch the children, because we cannot live together. I begin telling her that the fault is not mine and that she provoked me beyond endurance. She looks severely and solemnly at me and says: "Do not say any more, you will regret it." I tell her that I cannot stand comedies. Then she cries out something I don't catch, and rushes into her room. The key clicks behind her—she has locked herself in.

'I try the door, but getting no answer, go away angrily. Half-an-hour later Lisa runs in crying. "What is it? Has anything happened?" "We can't hear mama." We go. I pull at the double doors with all my might. The bolt had not been firmly secured, and the two halves both open. I approach the bed, on which she's lying awkwardly in her petticoats and with a pair of high boots on. An empty opium bottle is on the table. She is brought to herself. Tears follow, and a reconciliation. No, not a reconciliation: in the heart of each there is still the old animosity, with the additional irritation produced by the pain of this quarrel which each attributes to the other. But one must of course finish it all somehow, and life goes on in the old way. And so the same kind of quarrel, and even worse ones, occurred continually: once a week, once a month, or at times every day. It was always the same. Once I had already procured a passport to go abroad—the quarrel had continued for two days. But there was again a partial explanation, a partial reconciliation, and I didn't go.

XXI

'So those were our relations when that man appeared. He arrived in Moscow—his name is Trukhachevski—and came to my house. It was in the morning. I received him. We had once been on familiar terms and he tried to maintain a familiar tone by using non-committal expressions, but I definitely adopted a conventional tone and he at once submitted to it. I disliked him from the first glance. But curiously enough a strange and fatal force led me not to repel him, not to keep him away, but on the contrary to invite him to the house. After all, what could have been simpler than to converse with him coldly, and say goodbye without introducing him to my wife? But no, as if purposely, I began talking about his playing, and said I had been told he had given up the violin. He replied that, on the contrary, he now played more than ever. He referred to the fact that there had been a time when I myself played. I said I had given it up but that my wife played well. It is an astonishing thing that from the first day, from the first hour of my meeting him, my relations with him were such as they might have been only after all that subsequently happened. There was something strained in them: I noticed every word, every expression he or I used, and attributed importance to them.

'I introduced him to my wife. The conversation immediately turned to music, and he offered to be of use to her by playing with her. My wife was, as usual of late, very elegant, attractive, and disquietingly beautiful. He evidently pleased her at first sight. Besides she was glad that she would have someone to accompany her on a violin, which she was so fond of that she used to engage a violinist from the theatre for the purpose; and her face reflected her pleasure. But catching sight of me she at once understood my feeling and changed her expression, and a game of mutual deception began. I smiled pleasantly to appear as if I liked it. He, looking at my wife as all immoral men look at pretty women, pretended that he was only interested in the subject of the conversation—which no longer interested him at all; while she tried to seem indifferent, though my false smile of jealousy with which she was familiar, and his lustful gaze, evidently excited her. I saw that from their first encounter her eyes were particularly bright and, probably as a result of my jealousy, it seemed as if an electric current had been established between them, evoking as it were an identity of expressions, looks, and smiles. She blushed and he blushed. She smiled and he smiled. We spoke about music, Paris, and all sorts of trifles. Then he got up to go, and stood smilingly, holding his hat against his twitching thigh and looking now at her and now at me, as if in expectation of what we would do. I remember that instant just because at that moment I might not have invited him, and then nothing would have happened. But I glanced at him and at her and said silently to myself, "Don't suppose that I am jealous ... or that I am afraid of you," I added mentally addressing him, and I invited him to come some evening and bring his violin to play with my wife. She glanced at me with surprise, flushed, and as if frightened began to decline, saying that she did not play well enough. This refusal irritated me still more, and I insisted the more on his coming. I remember the curious feeling with which I looked at the back of his head, with the black hair parted in the middle contrasting with the white nape of his neck, as he went out with his peculiar springing gait suggestive of some kind of a bird. I couldn't conceal from myself that that man's presence tormented me. "It depends on me," I reflected, "to act so as to see nothing more of him. But that would be to admit that I am afraid of him. No, I am not afraid of him; it would be too humiliating," I said to myself. And there in the ante-room, knowing that my wife heard me, I insisted that he should come that evening with his violin. He promised to do so, and left.

'In the evening he brought his violin and they played. But it took a long time to arrange matters—they had not the music they wanted, and my wife could not without preparation play what they had. I was very fond of music and sympathized with their playing, arranging a music-stand for him and turning over the pages. They played a few things, some songs without words, and a little sonata by Mozart. They played splendidly, and he had an exceptionally fine tone. Besides that, he had a refined and elevated taste not at all in correspondence with his character.

'He was of course a much better player than my wife, and he helped her, while at the same time politely praising her playing. He behaved himself very well. My wife seemed interested only in music and was very simple and natural. But though I pretended to be interested in the music I was tormented by jealousy all the evening.

'From the first moment his eyes met my wife's I saw that the animal in each of them, regardless of all conditions of their position and of society, asked, "May I?" and answered, "Oh, yes, of course." I saw that he hadn't at all expected to find my wife, a Moscow lady, so attractive, and that he was very pleased. For he had no doubt whatever that she was *willing*. The only crux was whether that unendurable husband could hinder them. Had I been pure I wouldn't have understood this, but, like the majority of men, I had myself regarded women in that way before I married and therefore could read his mind like a manuscript. I was particularly tormented because I saw without doubt that she had no other feeling towards me than a continual irritation only occasionally interrupted by the habitual sensuality; but that this man—by his external refinement and novelty and still more by his undoubtedly great talent for music, by the nearness that comes of playing together, and by the influence music, especially the violin, exercises on impressionable natures—was sure not only to please but certainly and without the least hesitation to conquer, crush, bind her, twist her round his little finger and do whatever he liked with her.

'I could not help seeing this and I suffered terribly. But for all that, or perhaps on account of it, some force obliged me against my will to be not merely polite but amiable to him. Whether I did it for my wife or for him, to show that I was not afraid of him, or whether I did it to deceive myself—I don't know, but I know that from the first I could not behave naturally with him. In order not to yield to my wish to kill him there and then, I had to make much of him. I gave him expensive wines at supper, went into raptures over his playing, spoke to him with a particularly amiable smile, and invited him to dine and play with my wife again the next Sunday. I told him I would ask a few friends who were fond of music to hear him. And so it ended.'

Greatly agitated, Pozdnyshev changed his position and emitted his peculiar sound.

'It's strange how the presence of that man acted on me,' he began again, with an evident effort to keep calm. 'I come home from the Exhibition a day or two later, enter the ante-room, and suddenly feel something heavy, as if a stone had fallen on my heart, and I can't understand what it is. It was that passing through the ante-room I noticed something which reminded me of him. I realized what it was only in my study, and went back to the ante-room to make sure. Yes, I was not mistaken, there was his overcoat. A fashionable coat, you know. (Though I didn't realize it, I observed everything connected with him with extraordinary precision.) I inquire: sure enough he is there. I pass on to the dancing-room, not through the drawing-room but through the schoolroom. My daughter, Lisa, sits reading a book and the nurse sits with the youngest boy at the table, making a lid of some kind spin round. The door to the dancing-room is shut but I hear the sound of a rhythmic arpeggio and his and her voices. I listen, but can't make out anything.

'Evidently the sound of the piano is purposely made to drown the sound of their voices, their kisses ... perhaps. My God! What was aroused in me! Even to think of the beast that then lived in me fills me with horror! My heart suddenly contracted, stopped, and then began to beat like a hammer. My chief feeling, as usual whenever I was enraged, was one of self-pity. In the presence of the children! of their nanny! thought I. Probably I looked awful, for Lisa gazed at me with strange eyes. "What am I to do?" I asked myself. "Go in? I can't: heaven only knows what I should do. But neither can I go away." The nanny looked at me as if she understood my position. "But it's impossible not to go in," I said to myself, and I quickly opened the door. He was sitting at the piano playing those arpeggios with his large white upturned fingers. She was standing in the curve of the piano, bending over some open music. She was the first to see or hear, and glanced at me. Whether she was frightened and pretended not to be, or whether she was really not frightened, anyway she didn't start or move but only blushed, and that not at once.

' "How glad I am that you have come: we have not decided what to play on Sunday," she said in a tone she would not have used to me had we been alone. This and her using the word "we" of herself and him, filled me with indignation. I greeted him silently.

He pressed my hand, and at once, with a smile which I thought distinctly ironic, began to explain that he had brought some music to practise for Sunday, but that they disagreed about what to play: a classical but more difficult piece, namely Beethoven's sonata for the violin, or a few little pieces. It was all so simple and natural that there was nothing one could cavil at, yet I felt certain that it was all untrue and that they had agreed how to deceive me.

'One of the most distressing conditions of life for a jealous man (and everyone is jealous in our world) are certain society conventions which allow a man and a woman the greatest and most dangerous proximity. You would become a laughing-stock to others if you tried to prevent such nearness at balls, or the nearness of doctors to their women-patients, or of people occupied with art, sculpture, and especially music. A couple are occupied with the noblest of arts, music; this demands a certain nearness, and there is nothing reprehensible in that and only a stupid jealous husband can see anything undesirable in it. Yet everybody knows that it is by means of those very pursuits, especially of music, that the greater part of the adulteries in our society occur. I evidently confused them by the confusion I betrayed: for a long time I could not speak. I was like a bottle held upside down from which the water does not flow because it is too full. I wanted to abuse him and to turn him out, but again felt that I must treat him courteously and amiably. And I did so. I acted as though I approved of it all, and again because of the strange feeling which made me behave to him the more amiably the more his presence distressed me, I told him that I trusted his taste and advised her to do the same. He stayed as long as was necessary to efface the unpleasant impression caused by my sudden entrance—looking frightened and remaining silent—and then left, pretending that it was how decided what to play next day. I was however fully convinced that compared with what interested them the question of what to play was quite irrelevant.

'I saw him out to the ante-room with special politeness. (How could one do less than accompany a man who had come to disturb the peace and destroy the happiness of a whole family?) And I pressed his soft white hand with particular warmth.

XXII

'I didn't speak to her all that day—I couldn't. Nearness to her aroused in me such hatred of her that I was afraid of myself. At dinner in the presence of the children she asked me when I was going away. I had to go next week to the District Meetings of the Zemstvo. I told her the date. She asked whether I did not want anything for the journey. I did not answer but sat silent at table and then went in silence to my study. Latterly she used never to come to my room, especially not at that time of a day. I lay in my study filled with anger. Suddenly I heard her familiar step, and the terrible, monstrous idea entered my head that she, like Uriah's wife, wished to conceal the sin she had already committed and that that was why she was coming to me at such an unusual time. "Can she be coming to me?" thought I, listening to her approaching footsteps. "If she is coming here, then I am right," and an inexpressible hatred of her took possession of me. Nearer and nearer came the steps. Is it possible that she won't pass on to the dancing-room? No, the door creaks and in the doorway appears her shapely handsome figure, on her face and in her eyes a timid ingratiating look which she tries to hide, but which I see and the meaning of which I know. I almost choked, so long did I hold my breath, and still looking at her I clutched my cigarette-case and began to smoke.

' "Now how can you? One comes to sit with you for a bit, and you begin smoking"—and she sat down close to me on the sofa, leaning against me. I moved away so as not to touch her.

' "I see you are dissatisfied at my wanting to play on Sunday," she said.

' "I am not at all dissatisfied," I said.

' "As if I don't see!"

' "Well, I congratulate you on seeing. But I only see that you behave like a coquette. . . . You always find pleasure in all kinds of vileness, but to me it is terrible!"

' "Oh, well, if you are going to abuse me like a cabman I'll go away."

' "Do, but remember that if you don't value the family honour, I value not you (devil take you) but the honour of the family!"

' "But what is the matter? What?"

' "Go away, for God's sake be off!"

'Whether she pretended not to understand what it was about or really did not understand, at any rate she took offence, grew angry, and didn't go away but stood in the middle of the room.

' "You have really become impossible," she began. "You have a character that even an angel could not put up with." And as usual trying to sting me as painfully as possible, she reminded me of my conduct to my sister (an incident when, being exasperated, I said rude things to my sister); she knew I was distressed about it and she stung me just on that spot. "After that, nothing from you will surprise me," she said.

' "Yes! Insult me, humiliate me, disgrace me, and then put the blame on me," I said to myself, and suddenly I was seized by such terrible rage as I had never before experienced.

'For the first time I wished to give physical expression to that rage. I jumped up and went towards her; but just as I jumped up I remembered becoming conscious of my rage and asking myself: "Is it right to give way to this feeling?" and at once I answered that it was right, that it would frighten her, and instead of restraining my fury I immediately began fuelling it still further, and was glad it burnt yet more fiercely within me.

' "Be off, or I'll kill you!" I shouted, going up to her and seizing her by the arm. I consciously intensified the anger in my voice as I said this. And I suppose I was terrible, for she was so frightened that she had not even the strength to go away, but only said: "Vasya, what is it? What is the matter with you?"

' "Go!" I roared louder still. "No one but you can drive me to fury. I do not answer for myself!"

'Having given rein to my rage, I revelled in it and wished to do something still more unusual to show the extreme degree of my anger. I felt a terrible desire to beat her, to kill her, but knew that this wouldn't do, and so to give vent to my fury I seized a paper-weight from my table, again shouting "Go!" and hurled it to the floor near her. I aimed it very exactly past her. Then she left the room, but stopped at the doorway, and immediately, while she still saw it (I did it so that she might see), I began snatching things from the table—candlesticks and ink-stand—and hurling them on the floor still shouting "Go! Get out! I don't answer for myself!" She went away—and I immediately stopped.

'An hour later the nurse came to tell me that my wife was in hysterics. I went to her; she sobbed, laughed, could not speak, and her whole body was convulsed. She was not pretending, but was genuinely ill.

'Towards morning she grew quiet and we made peace under the influence of the feeling we called love.

'In the morning when, after our reconciliation, I confessed to her that I was jealous of Trukhachevski, she wasn't at all confused, but laughed most naturally; so strange did the very possibility of an infatuation for such a man seem to her, she said.

' "Could a decent woman have any other feeling for such a man than the pleasure of his music? Why, if you like I'm ready never to see him again . . . not even on Sunday, though everybody has been invited. Write and tell him that I am ill, and there's an end of it! Only it's unpleasant that anyone, especially he himself, should imagine that he is dangerous. I am too proud to allow anyone to think that of me!"

'And you know, she was not lying, she believed what she was saying; she hoped by those words to evoke in herself contempt for him and so to defend herself from him, but she did not succeed in doing so. Everything was against her, especially that accursed music. So it all ended, and on the Sunday the guests assembled and they again played together.

XXIII

'I suppose it is hardly necessary to say that I was very vain: if one isn't vain there is nothing to live for in our usual way of life. So on that Sunday I arranged the dinner and the musical evening with much care. I bought the provisions myself and invited the guests.

'Towards six the visitors assembled. He came in evening dress with diamond studs that showed bad taste. He behaved in a free and easy manner, answered everything hurriedly with a smile of agreement and understanding, you know, with that peculiar expression which seems to say that all you may do or say is just what he expected. Everything that was not in good taste about him I noticed with particular pleasure, because it ought all to have had the effect of tranquillizing me and showing that he was so far beneath my wife that, as she had said, she couldn't lower herself to his level. I did not now allow myself to be jealous. In the first place I had worried through that torment and needed rest, and secondly I wanted to believe my wife's assurances and did believe them. But though I was not jealous I was nevertheless not natural with either of them, and at dinner and during the first half of the evening before the music began I still followed their movements and looks.

'The dinner was, as dinners are, dull and pretentious. The music began pretty early. Oh, how I remember every detail of that evening! I remember how he brought in his violin, unlocked the case, took off the cover a lady had embroidered for him, drew out the violin, and began tuning it. I remember how my wife sat down at the piano with pretended unconcern, under which I saw that she was trying to conceal great timidity—chiefly as to her own ability—and then the usual A on the piano began, the *pizzicato* of the violin, and the arrangement of the music. Then I remember how they glanced at one another, turned to look at the audience who were seating themselves, said something to one another, and began. He took the first chords. His face grew serious, stern, and sympathetic, and listening to the sounds he produced, he touched the strings with careful figures. The piano answered him. The music began. . . .'

Pozdnyshev paused and produced his strange sound several times in succession. He tried to speak, but sniffed, and stopped.

'They played Beethoven's Kreutzer Sonata,' he continued. 'Do you know the first *presto*? You do?' he cried. 'Ugh! Ugh! It's a terrible thing, that sonata. And especially that part. And in general music is a dreadful thing! What is it? I don't understand it. What is music? What does it do? And why does it do what it does? They say music exalts the soul. Nonsense, it is not true! It has an effect, an awful effect—I am speaking of myself—but not of an exalting kind. It has neither an exalting nor a debasing effect but it produces agitation. How can I put it? Music makes me forget myself, my real position; it transports me to some other position not my own. Under the influence of music it seems to me that I feel what I do not really feel, that I understand what I do not understand, that I can do what I cannot do. I explain it by the fact that music acts like yawning, like laughter; I am not sleepy, but I yawn when I see someone yawning; there is nothing for me to laugh at, but I laugh when I hear people laughing.

'Music carries me immediately and directly into the mental condition in which the man was who composed it. My soul merges with his and together with him I pass from one condition into another, but why this happens I don't know. You see, he who wrote, let us say, the Kreutzer Sonata—Beethoven—knew of course why he was in that condition; that condition caused him to do certain actions and therefore that condition had a meaning for him, but for me—none at all. That is why music only agitates and doesn't lead to a conclusion. Well, when a military march is played the soldiers march to the music and the music has achieved its object. A dance is played, I dance and the music has achieved its object. Mass has been sung, I receive Communion, and that music too has reached a conclusion. Otherwise it's only agitating, and what ought to be done in that agitation is lacking. That is why music sometimes acts so dreadfully, so terribly. In China, music is a State affair. And that is as it should be. How can one allow anyone who pleases to hypnotize another, or many others, and do what he likes with them? And especially that this hypnotist should be the first immoral man who turns up?

'It's a terrible instrument in the hands of those who know how to use it! Take that Kreutzer Sonata, for instance, how can that first presto be played in a drawing-room among ladies in low-necked dresses? To hear that played, to clap a little, and then to eat ices and talk of the latest scandal? Such things should only be played on certain important significant occasions, and then only when certain actions answering to such music are wanted; play it then and do what the music has moved you to. Otherwise an awakening of energy and feeling unsuited both to the time and the place, to which no outlet is given, cannot but act harmfully. At any rate that piece had a terrible effect on me; it was as if quite new feelings, new possibilities, of which I had till then been unaware, had been revealed to me. "That's how it is: not at all as I used to think and live, but that way," something seemed to say within me. What this new thing was that had been revealed to me I could not explain to myself, but the consciousness of this new condition was very joyous. All those same people, including my wife and him, appeared in a new light.

'After that *allegro* they played the beautiful, but common and unoriginal, *andante* with trite variations, and the very weak *finale.* Then, at the request of the visitors, they played Ernst's Elegy and a few small pieces. They were all good, but they did not produce on me a one-hundredth part of the impression the first passage had. The effect of the first passage formed the background for them all.

'I felt light-hearted and cheerful the whole evening. I had never seen my wife as she was that evening. Those shining eyes, that severe, significant expression while she played, and her melting languor and feeble, pathetic, and blissful smile after they had finished. I saw all that but did not attribute any meaning to it except that she was feeling what I felt, and that to her as to me new feelings, never before experienced, were revealed or, as it were, recalled. The evening ended satisfactorily and the visitors departed.

'Knowing that I had to go away to attend the Zemstvo Meetings two days later, Trukhachevski on leaving said he hoped to repeat the pleasure of that evening when he next came to Moscow. From this I concluded that he did not consider it possible to come to my house during my absence, and this pleased me.

'It turned out that as I should not be back before he left town, we should not see one another again.

'For the first time I pressed his hand with real pleasure, and thanked him for the enjoyment he had given us. In the same way he bade a final farewell to my wife. Their leave-taking seemed to be most natural and proper. Everything was splendid. My wife and I were both very well satisfied with our evening party.

XXIV

'Two days later I left for the parish council meetings in the country, parting from my wife in the best and most tranquil of moods.

'In the district there was always an enormous amount to do and a quite special life, a special little world of its own. I spent two ten-hour days at the Council. A letter from my wife was brought me on the second day and I read it there and then.

'She wrote about the children, about uncle, about the nurse, about shopping, and among other things she mentioned, as a most natural occurrence, that Trukhachevski had called, brought some music he had promised, and had offered to play again, but that she had refused.

'I didn't remember his having promised any music, but thought he had taken leave for good, and I was therefore unpleasantly struck by this. I was however so busy that I had no time to think of it, and it was only in the evening when I had returned to my lodgings that I re-read her letter.

'Besides the fact that Trukhachevski had called at my house during my absence, the whole tone of the letter seemed to me unnatural. The mad beast of jealousy began to growl in its kennel and wanted to leap out, but I was afraid of that beast and quickly fastened him in. "What an abominable feeling this jealousy is!" I said to myself. "What could be more natural than what she writes?"

'I went to bed and began thinking about the affairs awaiting me next day. During those parish meetings, sleeping in a new place, I usually slept badly, but now I fell asleep very quickly. And as sometimes happens, you know, you feel a kind of electric shock and wake up. So I awoke thinking of her, of my physical love for her, and of Trukhachevski, and of everything being accomplished between them. Horror and rage gripped my heart. But I began to reason with myself. "What nonsense!" said I to myself. "There are no grounds to go on, there is nothing and there has been nothing. How can I so degrade her and myself as to imagine such horrors? He's a sort of hired violinist, known as a worthless fellow, and suddenly an honourable woman, the respected mother of a family, *my* wife.... What absurdity!" So it seemed to me on the one hand. "How could it help being so?" it seemed on the other. "How could that simplest and most intelligible thing help happening—that for the sake of which I married her, for the sake of which I have been living with her, what alone I wanted of her, and which others including this musician must therefore also want? He is an unmarried man, healthy (I remember how he crunched the gristle of a cutlet and how greedily his red lips clung to the glass of wine), well-fed, plump, and not merely unprincipled but evidently making it a principle to accept the pleasures that present themselves. And they have music, that most exquisite voluptuousness of the senses, as a link between them. What then could make him refrain? She? But who is she? She was, and still is, a mystery. I don't know her. I only know her as an animal. And nothing can or should restrain an animal."

'Only then did I remember their faces that evening when, after the Kreutzer Sonata, they played some impassioned little piece, I don't remember by whom, impassioned to the point of obscenity. "How dared I go away?" I asked myself, remembering their faces. Was it not clear that everything had happened between them that evening? Was it not evident already then that there was not only no barrier between them, but that they both, and she chiefly, felt a certain measure of shame after what had happened? I remember her weak, piteous, and beatific smile as she wiped the perspiration from her flushed face when I came up to the piano. Already then they avoided looking at one another, and only at supper when he was pouring out some water for her, they glanced at each other with the vestige of a smile. I now recalled with horror the glance and scarcely perceptible smile I had then caught. "Yes, it's all over," said one voice, and immediately the other voice said something entirely different. "Something has come over you, it can't be that it is so," said that other voice. It felt uncanny lying in the dark and I struck a light, and felt a kind of terror in that little room with its yellow wallpaper. I lit a cigarette and, as always happens when one's thoughts go round and round in a circle of insoluble contradictions, I smoked, taking one cigarette after another in order to befog myself so as not to see those contradictions.

'I didn't sleep all night, and at five in the morning, having decided that I couldn't continue in such a state of tension, I rose, woke the caretaker who attended me and sent him to get horses. I sent a note to the council saying that I had been recalled to Moscow on urgent business and asking that one of the members should take my place. At eight o'clock I got into my trap and started.'

XXV

The guard entered and seeing that our candle had burnt down put it out, without providing a fresh one. The day was dawning. Pozdnyshev was silent, but sighed deeply all the time the guard was in the carriage. He continued his story only after the guard had gone out, and in the semi-darkness of the carriage only the rattle of the windows of the moving carriage and the rhythmic snoring of the clerk could be heard. In the half-light of dawn I couldn't see Pozdnyshev's face at all, but only heard his voice becoming ever more and more agitated and full of suffering.

'I had to travel twenty-four miles by road and eight hours by rail. It was splendid driving. It was frosty autumn weather, bright and sunny. The roads were in that condition when the tyres leave their dark imprint on them, you know. They were smooth, the light brilliant, and the air invigorating. It was pleasant driving in the tarantass. When it grew lighter and I had started, I felt easier. Looking at the houses, the fields, and the passers-by, I forgot where I was going. Sometimes I felt that I was simply taking a drive, and that nothing of what was calling me back had taken place. This oblivion was peculiarly enjoyable. When I remembered where I was going to, I said to myself, "We shall see when the time comes; I won't think about it." When we were halfway an incident occurred which detained me and still further distracted my thoughts. The tarantass broke down and had to be repaired.

'That break-down had a very important effect, for it caused me to arrive in Moscow at midnight, instead of at seven o'clock as I had expected, and to reach home between twelve and one, as I missed the express and had to travel by a stopping train. Going to fetch a cart, having the tarantass mended, settling up, tea at the inn, a talk with the innkeeper—all this still further diverted my attention. It was twilight before all was ready and I started again. By night it was even pleasanter driving than during the day. There was a new moon, a slight frost, still good roads, good horses, and a jolly driver, and as I went on I enjoyed it, hardly thinking at all of what lay before me; or perhaps I enjoyed it just because I knew what awaited me and was saying goodbye to the joys of life. But that tranquil mood, that ability to suppress my feelings, ended with my drive. As soon as I entered the train something entirely different began. That eight-hour journey in a railway carriage was something dreadful, which I shall never forget all my life. Whether it was that having taken my seat in the carriage I vividly imagined myself as having already arrived, or that railway traveling has such an exciting effect on people, at any rate from the moment I sat down in the train I could no longer control my imagination, and with extraordinary vividness which inflamed my jealousy it painted incessantly, one after another, pictures of what had gone on in my absence, of how she had been false to me. I burnt with indignation, anger, and a peculiar feeling of intoxication with my own humiliation, as I gazed at those pictures, and I could not tear myself away from them; I could not help looking at them, could not efface them, and could not help evoking them.

'That wasn't all. The more I gazed at those imaginary pictures the stronger grew my belief in their reality. The vividness with which they presented themselves to me seemed to serve as proof that what I imagined was real. It was as if, against my will, some devil invented and suggested to me the most terrible reflections. An old conversation I had had with Trukhachevski's brother came to my mind, and in a kind of ecstasy I rent my heart with that conversation, making it refer to Trukhachevski and my wife.

'That had occurred long before, but I recalled it. Trukhachevski's brother, I remember, in reply to a question whether he frequented houses of ill-fame, had said that a decent man would not go to places where there was danger of infection and it was dirty and nasty, since he could always find a decent woman. And now his brother had found my wife! "True, she is not in her first youth, has lost a side-tooth, and there is a slight puffiness about her; but it can't be helped, one has to take what one can get," I imagined him to be thinking. "Yes, it's condescending of him to take her for his mistress!" I told myself. "And she's safe. . . . No, it is impossible!" I thought horror-struck. "There is nothing of the kind, nothing! There aren't even any grounds for suspecting such things. Didn't she tell me that the very thought that I could be jealous of him was degrading to her? Yes, but she is lying, she's always lying!" I exclaimed, and everything began anew. . . .

'There were only two other people in the carriage; an old woman and her husband, both very taciturn, and even they got out at one of the stations and I was quite alone. I was like a caged animal: now I jumped up and went to the window, now I began to walk up and down trying to speed the carriage up; but the carriage with all its seats and windows went jolting on in the same way, just as ours does. . . .'

Pozdnyshev jumped up, took a few steps, and sat down again.

'Oh, I am afraid, afraid of railway carriages, I'm seized with horror. Yes, it is awful!' he continued. 'I said to myself, "I will think of something else. Suppose I think of the innkeeper where I had tea," and there in my mind's eye appears the innkeeper with his long beard and his grandson, a boy of the age of my Vasya! He will see how the musician kisses his mother. What will happen in his poor soul? But what does she care? She loves . . ." and again the same thing rose up in me. "No, no . . . I will think about the inspection of the District Hospital. Oh, yes, about the patient who complained of the doctor yesterday. The doctor has a moustache like Trukhachevski's. And how impudent he is . . . they both deceived me when he said he was leaving Moscow," and it began afresh. Everything I thought of had some connection with them. I suffered dreadfully. The chief cause of the suffering was my ignorance, my doubt, and the contradictions within me: my not knowing whether I ought to love or hate her. My suffering was of a strange kind. I felt a hateful consciousness of my humiliation and of his victory, but a terrible hatred for her. "It will not do to put an end to myself and leave her; she must at least suffer to some extent, and at least understand that I have suffered," I said to myself. I got out at every station to divert my mind.

'At one station I saw some people drinking, and I immediately drank some vodka. Beside me stood a jew who was also drinking. He began to talk, and to avoid being alone in my carriage I went with him into his dirty third-class carriage reeking with smoke and bespattered with shells of sunflower seeds. There I sat down beside him and he chattered a great deal and told anecdotes. I listened to him, but could not take in what he was saying because I continued to think about my own affairs. He noticed this and demanded my attention. Then I rose and went back to my carriage. "I must think it over," I said to myself. "Is what I suspect true, and is there any reason for me to suffer?" I sat down, wishing to think it over calmly, but immediately, instead of calm reflection, the same thing began again: instead of reflection, pictures and fancies. "How often I have suffered like this," I said to myself (recalling former similar attacks of jealousy), "and afterwards it all ended in nothing. So it will be now perhaps, yes certainly it will. I shall find her calmly asleep, she will wake up, be pleased to see me, and by her words and looks I shall know that there has been nothing and that this is all nonsense. Oh, how good that would be! But no, that has happened too often and won't happen again now," some voice seemed to say; and it began again. Yes, that was where the punishment lay! I wouldn't take a young man to a lock-hospital to knock the hankering after women out of him, but into my soul, to see the devils that were rending it! What was terrible, you know, was that I considered myself to have a complete right to her body as if it were my own, and yet at the same time I felt I could not control that body, that it was not mine and she could dispose of it as she pleased, and that she wanted to dispose of it not as I wished her to. And I could do nothing either to her or to him. He, like Vanka the Steward, could sing a song before the gallows of how he kissed the sugared lips and so forth. And he would triumph. If she has not yet done it but wishes to—and I know that she does wish to—it is still worse; it would be better if she had done it and I knew it, so that there would be an end to this uncertainty. I could not have said what it was I wanted. I wanted her not to desire that which she was bound to desire. It was utter insanity.

XXVI

'At the last station but one, when the guard had been to collect the tickets, I gathered my things together and went out onto the brake-platform, and the consciousness that the crisis was at hand still further increased my agitation. I felt cold, and my jaw trembled so that my teeth chattered. I automatically left the terminus with the crowd, took a cab, got in, and drove off. I rode looking at the few passers-by, the night-watchmen, and the shadows of my trap thrown by the street lamps, now in front and now behind me, and didn't think of anything. When we had gone about half a mile my feet felt cold, and I remembered that I had taken off my woollen stockings in the train and put them in my satchel. "Where's the satchel? Is it here? Yes." And my wicker trunk? I remembered that I had entirely forgotten about my luggage, but finding that I had the luggage-ticket I decided that it was not worth while going back for it, and so continued my way.

'Try now as I will, I cannot recall my state of mind at the time. What did I think? What did I want? I don't know at all. All I remember is a consciousness that something dreadful and very important in my life was imminent. Whether that important event occurred because I thought it would, or whether I had a presentiment of what was to happen, I don't know. It may even be that after what has happened all the foregoing moments have acquired a certain gloom in my mind. I drove up to the front porch. It was past midnight. Some cabmen were waiting in front of the porch expecting, from the fact that there were lights in the windows, to pick up fares. (The lights were in our flat, in the dancing-room and drawing-room.)

'Without considering why it was still light in our windows so late, I went upstairs in the same state of expectation of something dreadful, and rang. Igor, a kind, willing, but very stupid footman, opened the door. The first thing my eyes fell on in the hall was a man's cloak hanging on the stand with other outdoor coats. I ought to have been surprised but was not, for I had expected it. "That's it!" I said to myself. When I asked Igor who the visitor was and he named Trukhachevski, I inquired whether there was anyone else. He replied, "Nobody, sir." I remember that he replied in a tone as if he wanted to cheer me and dissipate my doubts of there being anybody else there. "So it is, so it is," I seemed to be saying to myself. "And the children?" "All well, heaven be praised. In bed, long ago."

'I couldn't breathe, and couldn't check the trembling of my jaw. "Yes, so it's not as I thought: I used to expect a misfortune but things used to turn out all right and in the normal way. Now it's not as usual, but is all as I pictured to myself. I thought it was only fancy, but here it is, all real. Here it all is . . . !"

'I almost began to sob, but the devil immediately suggested to me: "Cry, be sentimental, and they will get away quietly. You will have no proof and will continue to suffer and doubt all your life." And my self-pity immediately vanished, and a strange sense of joy arose in me, that my torture would now be over, that now I could punish her, could get rid of her, and could vent my anger. And I gave vent to it—I became a beast, a cruel and cunning beast.

' "Don't!" I said to Igor, who was about to go to the drawing-room. "Here is my luggage-ticket, take a cab as quick as you can and go and get my luggage. Off you go!" He went down the passage to fetch his overcoat. Afraid that he might alarm them, I went as far as his little room and waited while he put on his overcoat. From the drawing-room, beyond another room, one could hear voices and the clatter of knives and plates. They were eating and hadn't heard the bell. "If only they don't come out now," thought I. Igor put on his overcoat, which had an astrakhan collar, and went out. I locked the door after him and felt creepy when I knew I was alone and must act at once. How, I did not yet know. I only knew that all was now over, that there could be no doubt as to her guilt, and that I should punish her immediately and end my relations with her.

'Previously I had doubted and had thought: "Perhaps after all it's not true, perhaps I'm mistaken." But now it was so no longer. It was all irrevocably decided. "Without my knowledge she is alone with him at night! That is a complete disregard of everything! Or worse still: it is intentional boldness and impudence in crime, that the boldness may serve as a sign of innocence. All is clear. There is no doubt." I only feared one thing—their parting hastily, inventing some fresh lie, and thus depriving me of clear evidence and of the possibility of proving the fact. So as to catch them more quickly I went on tiptoe to the dancing-room where they were, not through the drawing-room but through the passage and nurseries.

'In the first nursery slept the boys. In the second nursery the nurse moved and was about to wake, and I imagined to myself what she would think when she knew all; and such pity for myself seized me at that thought that I could not restrain my tears, and not to wake the children I ran on tiptoe into the passage and on into my study, where I fell sobbing on the sofa.

' "I, an honest man, I, the son of my parents, I, who have all my life dreamt of the happiness of married life; I, a man who was never unfaithful to her.... And now! Five children, and she is embracing a musician because he has red lips!

' "No, she's not a human being. She's a bitch, an abominable bitch! In the next room to her children whom she has all her life pretended to love. And writing to me as she did! Throwing herself so barefacedly on his neck! But what do I know? Perhaps she long ago carried on with the footmen, and so got the children who are considered mine!

' "Tomorrow I should have come back and she would have met me with her fine coiffure, with her elegant waist and her indolent, graceful movements" (I saw all her attractive, hateful face), "and that beast of jealousy would for ever have sat in my heart lacerating it. What will the nurse think? ... And Igor? And poor little Lisa! She already understands something. Ah, that impudence, those lies! And that animal sensuality which I know so well," I said to myself.

'I tried to get up but could not. My heart was beating so that I could not stand on my feet. "Yes, I shall die of a stroke. She will kill me. That is just what she wants. What is killing to her? But no, that would be too advantageous for her and I will not give her that pleasure. Yes, here I sit while they eat and laugh and ... Yes, though she was no longer in her first flush of youth he did not disdain her. For in spite of that she is not bad looking, and above all she is at any rate not dangerous to his precious health. And why did I not throttle her then?" I said to myself, recalling the moment when, the week before, I drove her out of my study and hurled things about. I vividly recalled the state I had then been in; I not only recalled it, but again felt the need to strike and destroy that I had felt then. I remember how I wished to act, and how all considerations except those necessary for action went out of my head. I entered into that condition when an animal or a man, under the influence of physical excitement at a time of danger, acts with precision and deliberation but without losing a moment and always with a single definite aim in view.

'The first thing I did was to take off my boots and, in my socks, approach the sofa, on the wall above which guns and daggers were hung. I took down a curved Damascus dagger that had never been used and was very sharp. I drew it out of its scabbard. I remember the scabbard fell behind the sofa, and I remember thinking "I must find it afterwards or it will get lost." Then I took off my overcoat which I was still wearing, and stepping softly in my socks I went ahead.

XXVII

'Having crept up stealthily to the door, I suddenly opened it. I remember the expression of their faces. I remember that expression because it gave me a painful pleasure—it was an expression of terror. That was just what I wanted. I shall never forget the look of desperate terror that appeared on both their faces the first instant they saw me. He I think was sitting at the table, but on seeing or hearing me he jumped to his feet and stood with his back to the cupboard. His face expressed nothing but quite unmistakable terror. Her face too expressed terror but there was something else besides. If it had expressed only terror, perhaps what happened might not have happened; but on her face there was, or at any rate so it seemed to me at the first moment, also an expression of regret and annoyance that love's raptures and her happiness with him had been disturbed. It was as if she wanted nothing but that her present happiness should not be interfered with. These expressions remained on their faces but an instant. The look of terror on his changed immediately to one of inquiry: might he, or might he not, begin lying? If he might, he must begin at once; if not, something else would happen. But what? . . . He looked inquiringly at her face. On her face the look of vexation and regret changed as she looked at him (so it seemed to me) to one of solicitude for him.

'For an instant I stood in the doorway holding the dagger behind my back.

'At that moment he smiled, and in a ridiculously indifferent tone remarked: "And we have been having some music."

'"What a surprise!" she began, falling into his tone. But neither of them finished; the same fury I had experienced the week before overcame me. Again I felt that need of destruction, violence, and a transport of rage, and yielded to it. Neither finished what they were saying. That something else began which he had feared and which immediately eliminated all they were saying. I rushed towards her, still hiding the dagger so that he might not prevent my striking her in the side under her breast. I selected that spot from the first. Just as I rushed at her he saw it, and—a thing I never expected of him—seized me by the arm and shouted: "Think what you are doing! . . . Help, someone! . . ."

'I snatched my arm away and rushed at him in silence. His eyes met mine and he suddenly grew as pale as a sheet to his very lips. His eyes flashed in a peculiar way, and—what again I had not expected—he darted under the piano and out at the door. I was going to rush after him, but a weight hung on my left arm. It was she. I tried to free myself, but she hung on yet more heavily and would not let me go. This unexpected hindrance, the weight, and her touch which was loathsome to me, inflamed me still more. I felt that I was quite mad and that I must look frightful, and this delighted me. I swung my left arm with all my might, and my elbow hit her straight in the face. She cried out and let go my arm. I wanted to run after him, but remembered that it's ridiculous to run after one's wife's lover in one's socks; and I didn't wish to be ridiculous but terrible. In spite of the fearful frenzy I was in, I was all the time aware of the impression I might produce on others, and was even partly guided by that impression. I turned towards her. She fell on the couch, and holding her hand to her bruised eyes, looked at me. Her face showed fear and hatred of me, the enemy, as a rat's does when one lifts the trap in which it has been caught. At any rate I saw nothing in her expression but this fear and hatred of me. It was just the fear and hatred of me which would be evoked by love for another. But still I might perhaps have restrained myself and not done what I did had she remained silent. But she suddenly began to speak and to catch hold of the hand in which I held the dagger.

' "Come to yourself! What are you doing? What's the matter? There has been nothing, nothing, nothing. . . . I swear it!"

'I might still have hesitated, but those last words of hers, from which I concluded just the opposite—that everything had happened—called forth a reply. And the reply had to correspond to the temper to which I had brought myself, which continued to increase and had to go on increasing. Fury, too, has its laws.

' "Don't lie, you wretch!" I howled, and seized her arm with my left hand, but she wrenched herself away. Then, still without letting go of the dagger, I seized her by the throat with my left hand, threw her backwards, and began throttling her. What a firm neck it was . . . ! She seized my hand with both hers trying to pull it away from her throat, and as if I had only waited for that, I struck her with all my might with the dagger in the side below the ribs.

'When people say they don't remember what they do in a fit of fury, it's rubbish, falsehood. I remembered everything and did not for a moment lose awareness of what I was doing. The more frenzied I became the more brightly the light of consciousness burnt in me, so that I could not help knowing everything I did. I knew what I was doing every second. I cannot say that I knew beforehand what I was going to do; but I knew what I was doing when I did it, and even I think a little before, as if to make repentance possible and to be able to tell myself that I could stop. I knew I was hitting below the ribs and that the dagger would enter. At the moment I did it I knew I was doing an awful thing such as I had never done before, which would have terrible consequences. But that consciousness passed like a flash of lightning and the deed immediately followed the consciousness. I realized the action with extraordinary clearness. I felt, and remember, the momentary resistance of her corset and of something else, and then the plunging of the dagger into something soft. She seized the dagger with her hands, and cut them, but could not hold it back.

'For a long time afterwards, in prison when the moral change had taken place in me, I thought of that moment, recalled what I could of it, and considered it. I remembered that for an instant, only an instant, before the action I had a terrible consciousness that I was killing, had killed, a defenceless woman, my wife! I remember the horror of that consciousness and conclude from that, and even dimly remember, that having plunged the dagger in I pulled it out immediately, trying to remedy what had been done and to stop it. I stood for a second motionless waiting to see what would happen, and whether it could be remedied.

'She jumped to her feet and screamed: "Nanny! He's killed me."

'Having heard the noise the nanny was standing by the door. I continued to stand waiting, and not believing the truth. But the blood rushed from under her corset. Only then did I understand that it could not be remedied, and I immediately decided that it wasn't necessary it should be, that I had done what I wanted and had to do. I waited till she fell down, and the nanny, crying "Good God!" ran to her, and only then did I throw away the dagger and leave the room.

'"I must not be excited; I must know what I am doing," I said to myself without looking at her and at the nanny. The nanny was screaming—calling for the maid. I went down the passage, sent the maid, and went into my study. "What am I to do now?" I asked myself, and immediately realized what it must be. On entering the study I went straight to the wall, took down a revolver and examined it—it was loaded—I put it on the table. Then I picked up the scabbard from behind the sofa and sat down there.

'I sat thus for a long time. I did not think of anything or call anything to mind. I heard the sounds of bustling outside. I heard someone drive up, then someone else. Then I heard and saw Igor bring into the room my wicker trunk he had fetched. As if anyone wanted that!

' "Have you heard what has happened?" I asked. "Tell the yard-porter to inform the police." He did not reply, and went away. I rose, locked the door, got out my cigarettes and matches and began to smoke. I had not finished the cigarette before sleep overpowered me. I must have slept for a couple of hours. I remember dreaming that she and I were friendly together, that we had quarrelled but were making it up, there was something rather in the way, but we were friends. I was awakened by someone knocking at the door. "That's the police!" I thought, waking up. "I have committed murder, I think. But perhaps it's *she,* and nothing has happened." There was again a knock at the door. I didn't answer, but was trying to solve the question whether it had happened or not. Yet, it had! I remembered the resistance of the corset and the plunging in of the dagger, and a cold shiver ran down my back. "Yes, it has. Yes, and now I must do away with myself too," I thought. But I thought this knowing that I should *not* kill myself. Still I got up and took the revolver in my hand. But it is strange: I remember how I had many times been near suicide, how even that day on the railway it had seemed easy, easy just because I thought how it would stagger her—now I was not only unable to kill myself but even to think of it. "Why should I do it?" I asked myself, and there was no reply. There was more knocking at the door. "First I must find out who is knocking. There will still be time for this." I put down the revolver and covered it with a newspaper. I went to the door and unlatched it. It was my wife's sister, a kindly, stupid widow. "Vasya, what is this?" and her ever ready tears began to flow.

' "What do you want?" I asked rudely. I knew I ought not to be rude to her and had no reason to be, but I could think of no other tone to adopt.

' "Vasya, she is dying! Ivan Zakharych says so." Ivan Zakharych was her doctor and adviser.

' "Is he here?" I asked, and all my animosity against her surged up again. "Well, what of it?"

' "Vasya, go to her. Oh, how terrible it is!" said she.

' "Shall I go to her?" I asked myself, and immediately decided that I must go to her. Probably it is always done, when a husband has killed his wife, as I had—he must certainly go to her. "If that is what is done, then I must go," I said to myself. "If necessary I shall always have time," I reflected, referring to the shooting of myself, and I went to her. "Now we shall have phrases, grimaces, but I will not yield to them," I thought. "Wait," I said to her sister, "it's silly without boots, let me at least put on slippers."

XXVIII

'Wonderful to say, when I left my study and went through the familiar rooms, the hope that nothing had happened again awoke in me; but the smell of that doctor's nastiness—iodoform and carbolic—took me aback. "No, it had happened." Going down the passage past the nursery I saw little Lisa. She looked at me with frightened eyes. It even seemed to me that all the five children were there and all looked at me. I approached the door, and the maid opened it from inside for me and passed out. The first thing that caught my eye was her light-grey dress thrown on a chair and all stained black with blood. She was lying on one of the twin beds (on mine because it was easier to get at), with her knees raised. She lay in a very sloping position supported by pillows, with her dressing jacket unfastened. Something had been put on the wound. There was a heavy smell of iodoform in the room. What struck me first and most of all was her swollen and bruised face, blue on part of the nose and under the eyes. This was the result of the blow with my elbow when she had tried to hold me back. There was nothing beautiful about her, but something repulsive as it seemed to me. I stopped on the threshold. "Go up to her, do," said her sister. "Yes, no doubt she wants to confess," I thought. "Shall I forgive her? Yes, she is dying and may be forgiven," I thought trying to be magnanimous. I went up close to her. She raised her eyes to me with difficulty, one of them was black, and with an effort said falteringly:

' "You've got your way, killed…" and through the look of suffering and even the nearness of death her face had the old expression of cold animal hatred that I knew so well. "I shan't … let you have … the children, all the same.… She (her sister) will take…"

'What to me was the most important matter, her guilt, her faithlessness, she seemed to consider it beneath her to speak of.

' "Yes, look and admire what you have done," she said looking towards the door, and she sobbed. In the doorway stood her sister with the children. "Yes, see what you have done."

'I looked at the children and at her bruised disfigured face, and for the first time I forgot myself, my rights, my pride, and for the first time saw a human being in her. And so insignificant did all that had offended me, all my jealousy, appear, and so important what I had done, that I wished to fall with my face to her hand, and say: "Forgive me," but dared not do so.

'She lay silent with her eyes closed, evidently too weak to say more. Then her disfigured face trembled and puckered. She pushed me feebly away.

' "Why did it all happen? Why?"

' "Forgive me," I said.

' "Forgive! That's all rubbish!… Only not to die!…" she cried, raising herself, and her glittering eyes were bent on me. "Yes, you have had your way!… I hate you! Ah! Ah!" she cried, evidently already in delirium and alarmed by something. "Shoot! I'm not afraid!… Only kill everyone…! He has gone…! Gone…!"

'After that the delirium continued all the time. She didn't

recognize anyone. She died towards noon that same day. Before that they had taken me to the police-station and from there to prison. There, during the eleven months I remained awaiting trial, I examined myself and my past, and understood it. I began to understand it on the third day: on the third day they took me *there* . . .'

He was by way of going on but, unable to repress his sobs, he stopped. When he recovered himself he continued:

'I only began to understand when I saw her in her coffin. . .'

He gave a sob, but immediately continued hurriedly:

'Only when I saw her dead face did I understand all that I had done. I realized that I had killed her; that it was my doing that she, living, moving, warm, had now become motionless, waxen, and cold, and that this could never, anywhere or by any means, be remedied. He who has not lived through it cannot understand. . . . Oh! Oh! Oh! . . .' he cried several times and then was silent.

We sat in silence a long while. He kept sobbing and trembling as he sat opposite me without speaking. His face had grown narrow and elongated and his mouth seemed to stretch right across it.

'Yes,' he suddenly said. 'Had I then known what I know now, everything would have been different. Nothing would have induced me to marry her. . . . I should not have married at all.'

Again we remained silent for a long time.

'Well, forgive me. . . .' He turned away from me and lay down on the seat, covering himself up with his rug. At the station where I had to get out (it was at eight o'clock in the morning) I went up to him to say goodbye. Whether he was asleep or only pretended to be, at any rate he did not move. I touched him with my hand. He uncovered his face, and I could see he has not been asleep.

'Goodbye,' I said, holding out my hand. He gave me his and smiled slightly, but so piteously that I felt ready to weep.

'Yes, forgive me. . .' he said, repeating the same words with which he had concluded his story.

Father Sergius
[1898]

I

In Petersburg in the eighteen-forties a surprising event occurred. An officer of the Cuirassier Life Guards, a handsome prince who everyone predicted would become aide-de-camp to the Emperor Nicholas I and have a brilliant career, left the service, broke off his engagement to a beautiful maid of honour, a favourite of the Empress's, gave his small estate to his sister, and retired to a monastery to become a monk.

This event appeared extraordinary and inexplicable to those who did not know his inner motives, but for Prince Stepan Kasatsky himself it all occurred so naturally that he could not imagine how he could have acted otherwise.

His father, a retired colonel of the Guards, had died when Stepan was twelve, and sorry as his mother was to part from her son, she entered him at the Military College as her deceased husband had intended.

The widow herself, with her daughter Varvara, moved to Petersburg to be near her son and have him with her for the holidays.

The boy was distinguished both by his brilliant ability and by his immense self-esteem. He was first both in his studies—especially in mathematics, of which he was particularly fond—and also in drill and in riding. Though of more than average height, he was handsome and agile, and he would have been an altogether exemplary cadet had it not been for his quick temper. He was remarkably truthful, and was neither dissipated nor addicted to drink. The only faults that marred his conduct were fits of fury to which he was subject and during which he lost control of himself and became like a wild animal. He once nearly threw out of the window another cadet who had begun to tease him about his collection of minerals. On another occasion he came almost completely to grief by flinging a whole dish of cutlets at an officer who was acting as steward, attacking him and, it was said, striking him for having broken his word and told a blatant lie. He would certainly have been reduced to the ranks had not the Director of the College hushed up the whole matter and dismissed the steward.

By the time he was eighteen he had finished his College course and received a commission as lieutenant in an aristocratic regiment of the Guards.

The Emperor Nicholas Pavlovich (Nicholas I) had noticed him while he was still at the College, and continued to take notice of him in the regiment, and it was on this account that people predicted for him an appointment as aide-de-camp to the Emperor. Kasatsky himself strongly desired it, not from ambition only but chiefly because since his cadet days he had been passionately devoted to Nicholas Pavlovich. The Emperor had often visited the Military College and every time Kasatsky saw that tall erect figure, with breast expanded in its military overcoat, entering with brisk step, saw the cropped side-whiskers, the moustache, the aquiline nose, and heard the sonorous voice exchanging greetings with the cadets, he was seized by the same rapture that he experienced later on when he met the woman he loved. Indeed, his passionate adoration of the Emperor was even stronger: he wished to sacrifice something—everything, even himself—to prove his complete devotion. The Emperor Nicholas was conscious of evoking this rapture and deliberately aroused it. He played with the cadets, surrounded himself with them, treating them sometimes with childish simplicity, sometimes as a friend, and then again with majestic solemnity. After that affair with the officer, Nicholas Pavlovich said nothing to Kasatsky, except that when the latter approached he waved him away theatrically, frowned, shook his finger at him, and afterwards when leaving, said: 'Remember that I know everything. There are some things I would rather not know, but they remain here,' and he pointed to his heart.

When on leaving College the cadets were received by the Emperor, he did not again refer to Kasatsky's misdemeanor, but told them all, as was his custom, that they should serve him and the fatherland loyally, that he would always be their best friend, and that when necessary they might approach him direct. All the cadets were as usual greatly moved, and Kasatsky even shed tears, remembering the past, and vowed that he would serve his beloved Tsar with all his soul.

When Kasatsky took up his commission his mother moved with her daughter first to Moscow and then to their country estate. Kasatsky gave half his property to his sister and kept only enough to maintain himself in the expensive regiment he had joined.

To all appearance he was just an ordinary, brilliant young officer of the Guards making a career for himself; but intense and complex strivings went on within him. From early childhood his efforts had seemed to be very varied, but essentially they were all one and the same. He tried in everything he took up to attain such success and perfection as would evoke praise and surprise. Whether it was his studies or his military exercises, he took them up and worked at them till he was praised and held up as an example to others. Mastering one subject he took up another, and obtained first place in his studies. For example, while still at College he noticed in himself an awkwardness in French conversation, and contrived to master French till he spoke it as well as Russian; then he took up chess and became an excellent player.

Apart from his main vocation, which was the service of his Tsar and the fatherland, he always set himself some particular aim, and however unimportant it was, devoted himself completely to it and lived for it until it was accomplished. And as soon as it was attained another aim would immediately present itself, replacing its predecessor. This passion for distinguishing himself, or for accomplishing something in order to distinguish himself, filled his life. On taking up his commission he set himself to acquire the utmost perfection in knowledge of the service, and very soon became a model officer, though still with the same fault of ungovernable irascibility, which here in the service again led him to commit actions inimical to his success. Then he took to reading, having once in conversation in society felt himself deficient in general education—and again achieved his purpose. Then, wishing to secure a brilliant position in high society, he learnt to dance excellently and very soon was invited to all the balls in the best circles, and to some of their evening gatherings. But this did not satisfy him: he was accustomed to being first, and in such society was far from being so.

The highest society then consisted—and I think always and everywhere does consist—of four sorts of people: rich people who are received at Court, people not wealthy but born and brought up in Court circles, rich people who ingratiate themselves into the Court set, and people neither rich nor belonging to the Court but who ingratiate themselves into the first and second sets.

Kasatsky did not belong to the first two sets, but was readily welcomed in the others. On entering society he determined to have relations with some society lady, and to his own surprise quickly accomplished this purpose. He soon realized, however, that the circles in which he was moving were not the highest, and that though he was received in the highest spheres he did not belong to them. They were gracious to him, but showed by their whole manner that they had their own set and that he was not of it. Kasatsky wished to belong to that inner circle. To attain that end it would be necessary to be an aide-de-camp to the Emperor—which he expected to become—or to marry into that exclusive set, which he resolved to do.

His choice fell on a beauty belonging to the Court, who not merely belonged to the circle into which he wished to be accepted, but whose friendship was coveted by the very highest people and those most firmly established in that highest circle. This was Countess Korotkova. Kasatsky began to pay court to her, and not merely for the sake of his career. She was extremely attractive and he soon fell in love with her. At first she was noticeably cool towards him, but then suddenly changed and became amiable, and her mother gave him pressing invitations to visit them. Kasatsky proposed and was accepted. He was surprised at the facility with which he attained such happiness. But though he noticed something strange and unusual in the behaviour towards him of both mother and daughter, he was blinded by being so deeply in love, and did not realize what almost the whole town knew—namely, that his fiancée had been the Emperor Nicholas's mistress the previous year.

Two weeks before the day arranged for the wedding, Kasatsky was at Tsarskoe Selo at his fiancée's country place. It was a hot day in May. He and his betrothed had walked about the garden and were sitting on a bench in a shady linden alley. Mary's white muslin dress suited her particularly well, and she seemed the personification of innocence and love as she sat, now bending her head, now gazing up at the very tall and handsome man who was speaking to her with particular tenderness and self-restraint, as if he feared by word or gesture to offend or sully her angelic purity.

Kasatsky belonged to those men of the eighteen-forties (they are now no longer to be found) who while deliberately and without any conscientious scruples condoning impurity in themselves, required ideal and angelic purity in their women, regarded all unmarried women of their circle as possessed of such purity, and treated them accordingly. There was much that was false and harmful in this outlook, as concerning the laxity the men permitted themselves, but in regard to the women that old-fashioned view (sharply differing from that held by young people today who see in every girl merely a female seeking a mate) was, I think, of value. The girls, perceiving such adoration, endeavoured with varying degrees of success to be goddesses.

Such was the view Kasatsky held of women, and that was how he regarded his fiancée. He was particularly in love that day, but did not experience any sensual desire for her. On the contrary he regarded her with tender adoration as something unattainable.

He rose to his full height, standing before her with both hands on his sabre.

'I have only now realized what happiness a man can experience! And it is you, my darling, who have given me this happiness,' he said with a timid smile.

Endearments had not yet become usual between them, and feeling himself morally inferior he felt terrified at this stage to use them to such an angel.

'It is thanks to you that I have come to know myself. I have learnt that I am better than I thought.'

'I have known that for a long time. That was why I began to love you.'

Nightingales trilled near by and the fresh leafage rustled, moved by a passing breeze.

He took her hand and kissed it, and tears came into his eyes.

She understood that he was thanking her for having said she loved him. He silently took a few steps up and down, and then approached her again and sat down.

'You know . . . I have to tell you . . . I was not disinterested when I began to pay court to you. I wanted to get into society; but later . . . how unimportant that became in comparison with you—when I got to know you. You are not angry with me for that?'

She did not reply but merely touched his hand. He understood that this meant: 'No, I am not angry.'

'You said . . .' He hesitated. It seemed too bold to say. 'You said that you began to love me. I believe it—but there is something that troubles you and checks your feeling. What is it?'

'Yes—now or never!' thought she. 'He is bound to know of it anyway. But now he will not forsake me. Ah, if he should, it would he terrible!' And she threw a loving glance at his tall, noble, powerful figure. She loved him now more than she had loved the Tsar, and apart from the Imperial dignity would not have preferred the Emperor to him.

'Listen! I cannot deceive you. I have to tell you. You ask what it is? It is that I have loved before.'

She again laid her hand on his with an imploring gesture. He was silent.

'You want to know who it was? It was—the Emperor.'

'We all love him. I can imagine you, a schoolgirl at the Institute . . .'

'No, it was later. I was infatuated, but it passed . . . I must tell you . . .'

'Well, what of it?'

'No, it was not simply—' She covered her face with her hands.

'What? You gave yourself to him?'

She was silent.

'His mistress?'

She did not answer.

He sprang up and stood before her with trembling jaws, pale as death. He now remembered how the Emperor, meeting him on the Nevsky, had amiably congratulated him.

'O God, what have I done! Stiva!'

'Don't touch me! Don't touch me! Oh, how it pains!'

He turned away and went to the house. There he met her mother.

'What is the matter, Prince? I . . .' She became silent on seeing his face. The blood had suddenly rushed to his head.

'You knew it, and used me to shield them! If you weren't a woman . . . !' he cried, lifting his enormous fist, and turning aside he ran away.

Had his fiancée's lover been a private person he would have killed him, but it was his beloved Tsar.

Next day he applied both for furlough and his discharge, and professing to be ill, so as to see no one, he went off to the country.

He spent the summer at his village arranging his affairs. When summer was over he did not return to Petersburg, but entered a monastery and there became a monk.

His mother wrote to try to dissuade him from this decisive step, but he replied that he felt God's call which transcended all other considerations. Only his sister, who was as proud and ambitious as he, understood him.

She understood that he had become a monk in order to be above those who considered themselves his superiors. And she understood him correctly. By becoming a monk he showed contempt for all that seemed most important to others and had seemed so to him too while he was in the service; and he now ascended to a height from which he could look down on those he had formerly envied. . . . But it was not this alone, as his sister Varvara supposed, that influenced him. There was also in him something else—a sincere religious feeling which Varvara did not know, which intertwined itself with the feeling of pride and the desire for pre-eminence, and guided him. His disillusionment with Mary, whom he had thought of angelic purity, and his sense of injury, were so strong that they brought him to despair, and the despair led him—to what? To God, to his childhood faith which had never been destroyed in him.

II

Kasatsky entered the monastery on the feast of the Intercession of the Blessed Virgin. The Abbot of that monastery was a gentleman by birth, a learned writer and a *stárets,* that is, he belonged to that succession of monks originating in Walachia who each choose a director and teacher whom they implicitly obey. This Superior had been a disciple of the *stárets* Ambrose, who was a disciple of Makarius, who was a disciple of the *stárets* Leonid, who was a disciple of Paissy Velichkovsky.

To this Abbot Kasatsky submitted himself as to his chosen director. Here in the monastery, besides the feeling of ascendency over others that such a life gave him, he felt much as he had done in the world: he found satisfaction in attaining the greatest possible perfection outwardly as well as inwardly. As in the regiment he had been not merely an irreproachable officer but had even exceeded his duties and widened the borders of perfection, so also a monk he tried to be perfect, and was always industrious, abstemious, submissive, and meek, as well as pure both in deed and in thought, and obedient. This last quality in particular made life far easier for him. If many of the demands of life in the monastery, which was near the capital much frequented, did not please him and were temptations to him, they were all nullified by obedience: 'It is not for me to reason; my business is to do the task set me, whether it be standing beside the relics, singing in the choir, or making up accounts in the monastery guest-house.'

All possibility of doubt about anything was silenced by obedience to the *stárets*. Had it not been for this, he would have been oppressed by the length and monotony of the church services, the bustle of the many visitors, and the bad qualities of the other monks. As it was, he not only bore it all joyfully but found in it solace and support. 'I don't know why it is necessary to hear the same prayers several times a day, but I know that it is necessary; and knowing this I find joy in them.' His director told him that as material food is necessary for the maintenance of the life of the body, so spiritual food—the church prayers—is necessary for the maintenance of the spiritual life. He believed this, and though the church services, for which he had to get up early in the morning, were a difficulty, they certainly calmed him and gave him joy. This was the result of his consciousness of humility, and the certainty that whatever he had to do, being fixed by the *stárets*, was right.

The interest of his life consisted not only in an ever greater and greater subjugation of his will, but in the attainment of all the

Christian virtues, which at first seemed to him easily attainable. He had given his whole estate to his sister and did not regret it, he had no personal claims, humility towards his inferiors was not merely easy for him but afforded him pleasure. Even victory over the sins of the flesh, greed and lust, was easily attained. His director had specially warned him against the latter sin, but Kasatsky felt free from it and was glad.

One thing only tormented him—the remembrance of his fiancée; and not merely the remembrance but the vivid image of what might have been. Involuntarily he recalled a lady he knew who had been a favourite of the Emperor's, but had afterwards married and become an admirable wife and mother. The husband had a high position, influence and honour, and a good and penitent wife.

In his better hours Kasatsky was not disturbed by such thoughts, and when he recalled them at such times he was merely glad to feel that the temptation was past. But there were moments when all that made up his present life suddenly grew dim before him, moments when, if he did not cease to believe in the aims he had set himself, he ceased to see them and could evoke no confidence in them but was seized by a remembrance of, and—terrible to say—a regret for, the change of life he had made.

The only thing that saved him in that state of mind was obedience and work, and the fact that the whole day was occupied by prayer. He went through the usual forms of prayer, he bowed in prayer, he even prayed more than usual, but it was lip-service only and his soul was not in it. This condition would continue for a day, or sometimes for two days, and would then pass of itself. But those days were dreadful. Kasatsky felt that he was neither in his own hands nor in God's, but was subject to something else. All he could do then was to obey the *stárets,* to restrain himself, to undertake nothing, and simply to wait. In general all this time he lived not by his own will but by that of the *stárets,* and in this obedience he found a special tranquillity.

So he lived in his first monastery for seven years. At the end of the third year he received the tonsure and was ordained to the priesthood by the name of Sergius. The profession was an important event in his inner life. He had previously experienced a great consolation and spiritual exaltation when receiving communion, and now when he himself officiated, the performance of the preparation filled him with ecstatic and deep emotion. But subsequently that feeling became more and more deadened, and once when he was officiating in a depressed state of mind he felt that the influence produced on him by the service would not endure. And it did in fact weaken till only the habit remained.

In general in the seventh year of his life in the monastery Sergius grew weary. He had learnt all there was to learn and had attained all there was to attain, there was nothing more to do and his spiritual drowsiness increased. During this time he heard of his mother's death and his sister Varvara's marriage, but both events were matters of indifference to him. His whole attention and his whole interest were concentrated on his inner life.

In the fourth year of his priesthood, during which the Bishop had been particulary kind to him, the *stárets* told him that he ought not to decline it if he were offered an appointment to higher duties. Then monastic ambition, the very thing he had found so repulsive in other monks, arose within him. He was assigned to a monastery near the metropolis. He wished to refuse but the *stárets* ordered him to accept the appointment. He did so, and took leave of the *stárets* and moved to the other monastery.

The exchange into the metropolitan monastery was an important even in Sergius's life. There he encountered many temptations, and his whole will-power was concentrated on meeting them.

In the first monastery, women had not been a temptation to him, but here that temptation arose with terrible strength and even took definite shape. There was a lady known for her frivolous behaviour who began to seek his favour. She talked to him and asked him to visit her. Sergius sternly declined, but was horrified by the definiteness of his desire. He was so alarmed that he wrote about it to the *stárets*. And in addition, to keep himself in hand, he spoke to a young novice and, conquering his sense of shame, confessed his weakness to him, asking him to keep watch on him and not let him go anywhere except to service and fulfil his duties.

Besides this, a great pitfall for Sergius lay in the fact of his extreme antipathy to his new Abbot, a cunning worldly man who was making a career for himself in the church. Struggle with himself as he might, he could not master that feeling. He was submissive to the Abbot, but in the depths of his soul he never ceased to condemn him. And in the second year of his residence at the new monastery that ill-feeling broke surface.

The Vigil service was being performed in the large church on the eve of the feast of the Intercession of the Blessed Virgin, and there were many visitors. The Abbot himself was conducting the service. Father Sergius was standing in his usual place and praying: that is, he was in that condition of struggle which always occupied him during the service, especially in the large church when he was not himself conducting the service. This conflict was occasioned by his irritation at the presence of fine folk, especially ladies. He tried not to see them or to notice all that went on: how a soldier conducted them, pushing the common people aside, how the ladies pointed out monks to one another—especially himself and a monk noted for his good looks. He tried as it were to keep his mind in blinkers, to see nothing but the light of the candles on the altar-screen, the icons, and those conducting the service. He tried to hear nothing but the prayers that were being chanted or read, to feel nothing but self-oblivion in consciousness of the fulfilment of duty—a feeling he always experienced when hearing or reciting in advance the prayers he had so often heard.

So he stood, crossing and prostrating himself when necessary, and struggled with himself, now giving way to cold condemnation and now to a consciously evoked obliteration of thought and feeling. Then the sacristan, Father Nicodemus—also a great stumbling-block to Sergius who involuntarily reproached him for flattering and fawning on the Abbot—approached him and, bowing low, requested his presence behind the holy gates. Father Sergius straightened his mantle, put on his biretta, and went circumspectly through the crowd.

'*Lise, regarde à droite, c'est lui!*' he heard a woman's voice say.

'*Où, où? Il n'est pas tellement beau.*'

He knew that they were speaking of him. He heard them and, as always, at moments of temptation, he repeated the words, 'Lead us not into temptation', and bowing his head and lowering his eyes went past the ambo and in by the north door, avoiding the canons in their cassocks who were just then passing the altar-screen. On entering the sanctuary he bowed, crossing himself as usual and bending double before the icons. Then, raising his head but without turning, he glanced out of the corner of his eye at the Abbot, whom he saw standing beside another glittering figure.

The Abbot was standing by the wall in his vestments. Having freed his little plump hands from beneath his chasuble he had folded them over his fat paunch, and fingering the cords of his vestments was smilingly saying something to a military man in the uniform of a general of the Imperial suite, with its insignia and shoulder-knots which Father Sergius's experienced eye instantly recognized. This general had been the commander of the regiment in which Sergius had served. He now evidently occupied an important position, and Father Sergius at once noticed that the Abbot was aware of this and that his red face and bald head beamed with satisfaction and pleasure. This vexed and disgusted Father Sergius, the more so when he heard that the Abbot had sent for him only to satisfy the general's curiosity to see a man who had formerly 'served with him', as he expressed it.

'Very pleased to see you in your angelic guise,' said the general, holding out his hand, 'I hope you have not forgotten an old comrade.'

The whole thing—the Abbot's red, smiling face amid its fringe of grey, the general's words, his well-cared-for face with its self-satisfied smile and the smell of wine from his breath and of cigars from his whiskers—revolted Father Sergius. He bowed again to the Abbot and said:

'Your reverence deigned to send for me?'—and stopped, the whole expression of his face and eyes asking why.

'Yes, to meet the General,' replied the Abbot.

'Your reverence, I left the world to save myself from temptation,' said Father Sergius, turning pale and with quivering lips. 'Why do you expose me to it during prayers and in God's house?'

'You may go! Go!' said the Abbot, flaring up and frowning.

Next day Father Sergius asked pardon of the Abbot and of the brethren for his pride, but at the same time, after a night spent in prayer, he decided that he must leave this monastery, and he wrote to the *stárets* begging permission to return to him. He wrote that he felt his weakness and incapacity to struggle against temptation without his help, and penitently confessed his sin of pride. By return of post came a letter from the *stárets,* who wrote that Sergius's pride was the cause of all that had happened. The old man pointed out that his fits of anger were due to the fact that in refusing all clerical honours he humiliated himself not for the sake of God but for the sake of his pride. 'There now, am I not a splendid man not to want anything?' That was why he could not tolerate the Abbot's action. 'I have renounced everything for the glory of God, and here I am exhibited like a wild beast!' 'Had you renounced vanity for God's sake you would have borne it. Worldly pride is not yet dead in you. I have thought about you, Sergius my son, and prayed also, and this is what God has suggested to me. At the Tambov hermitage the anchorite Hilary, a man of saintly life, has died. He had lived there eighteen years. The Tambov Abbot is asking whether there is not a brother who would take his place. And here comes your letter. Go to Father Paissy of the Tambov Monastery. I will write to him about you, and you must ask for Hilary's cell. Not that you can replace Hilary, but you need solitude to quell your pride. May God bless you!'

Sergius obeyed the *stárets*, showed his letter to the Abbot, and having obtained his permission, gave up his cell, handed all this possessions over to the monastery, and set out for the Tambov hermitage.

There the Abbot, an excellent manager of merchant origin, received Sergius simply and quietly and placed him in Hilary's cell, at first assigning to him a lay brother but afterwards leaving him alone, at Sergius's own request. The cell was a dual cave, dug into the hillside, and in it Hilary had been buried. In the back part was Hilary's grave, while in the front was a niche for sleeping, with a straw mattress, a small table, and a shelf with icons and books. Outside the outer door, which fastened with a hook, was another shelf on which, once a day, a monk placed food from the monastery.

And so Sergius became a hermit.

III

At Carnival time, in the sixth year of Sergius's life at the hermitage, a merry company of rich people, men and women from a neighbouring town, made up a troika party, after a meal of carnival pancakes and wine. The company consisted of two lawyers, a wealthy landowner, an officer, and four ladies. One lady was the officer's wife, another wife of the landowner, the third his sister— a young girl—and the fourth a divorcée, beautiful, rich, and eccentric, who amazed and shocked the town with her escapades.

The weather was excellent and the snow-covered road smooth as a floor. They drove some seven miles out of town, and then stopped and consulted as to whether they should turn back or drive farther.

'But where does this road lead to?' asked Makovkina, the beautiful divorcée.

'To Tambov, eight miles from here,' replied one of the lawyers, who was having a flirtation with her.

'And then where?'

'Then on to L——, past the Monastery.'

'Where that Father Sergius lives?'

'Yes.'

'Kasatsky, the handsome hermit?'

'Yes.'

'*Mesdames and messieurs,* let us drive on and see Kasatsky! We can stop at Tambov and have something to eat.'

'But we shouldn't get home tonight!'

'Never mind, we will stay at Kasatsky's.'

'Well, there is a very good hostelry at the Monastery. I stayed there when I was defending Makhin.'

'No, I shall spend the night at Kasatsky's!'

'Impossible! Even your omnipotence could not accomplish that!'

'Impossible? Will you bet?'

'All right! If you spend the night with him, the stake shall be whatever you like.'

'*A discrétion!*'

'But on your side too!'

'Yes, of course, Let us drive on.'

Vodka was handed to the drivers, and the party got out a box of pies, wine, and sweets for themselves. The ladies wrapped up in their white dogskins. The drivers disputed as to whose troika should go ahead, and the youngest, seating himself sideways with a dashing air, swung his long knout and shouted to the horses.

The troika-bells tinkled and the sledge-runners squeaked over the snow.

The sledges swayed hardly at all. The shaft-horse, with his tightly bound tail under his decorated breechband, galloped smoothly and briskly; the smooth road seemed to run rapidly behind them, while the driver dashingly shook the reins. One of the lawyers and the officer sitting opposite talked nonsense to Makovkina's neighbour, but Makovkina herself sat motionless and in thought, tightly wrapped in her fur. 'Always the same and always nasty! The same red shiny faces smelling of wine and cigars! The same talk, the same thoughts, and always about the same things! And they are all satisfied and confident that it should be so, and will go on living like that till they die. But I can't. It bores me. I want something that would upset it all and turn it upside down. Suppose it happened to us as to those people—at Saratov was it?—who kept on driving and froze to death.... What would our people do? How would they behave? Basely, for certain. Each for himself. And I too should act badly. But I at any rate have beauty. They all know it. And how about that monk? Is it possible that he has become indifferent to it? No! That is the one thing they all care for—like that cadet last autumn. What a fool he was!'

'Ivan Nikolaevich!' she said aloud.

'What are your commands?'

'How old is he?'

'Who?'

'Kasatsky.'

'Over forty, I should think.'

'And does he receive all visitors?'

'Yes, everybody, but not always.'

'Cover up my feet. Not like that—how clumsy you are! No! More, more—like that! But you need not squeeze them!'

So they came to the forest where the cell was.

Makovkina got out of the sledge, and told them to drive on.

They tried to dissuade her, but she grew irritable and ordered them to go on.

When the sledges had gone she went up the path in her white dogskin coat. The lawyer got out and stopped to watch her.

It was Father Sergius's sixth year as a recluse, and he was now forty-nine. His life in solitude was hard—not on account of the fasts and the prayers (they were no hardship to him) but on account of an inner conflict he had not at all anticipated. The sources of that conflict were two: doubts, and the lust of the flesh. And these two enemies always appeared together. It seemed to him that they were two foes, but in reality they were one and the same. As soon as doubt was gone so was the lustful desire. But thinking them to be two different fiends he fought them separately.

'O my God, my God!' thought he. 'Why dost thou not grant me faith? There is lust, of course: even the saints had to fight that—Saint Anthony and others. But they had faith, while I have moments, hours, and days, when it is absent. Why does the whole world, with all its delights, exist if it is sinful and must be renounced? Why hast Thou created this temptation? Temptation? Is it not rather a temptation that I wish to abandon all the joys of earth and prepare something for myself there where perhaps there is nothing?' And he became horrified and filled with disgust at himself. 'Vile creature! And it is you who wish to become a saint!' he upbraided himself, and he began to pray. But as soon as he started to pray he saw himself vividly as he had been at the Monastery, in a majestic that is not right. It is deception. I may deceive others, but not myself or God. I am not a majestic man, but a pitiable and ridiculous one!' And he threw back the folds of his cassock and smiled as he looked at his thin legs in their underclothing.

Then he dropped the folds of the cassock again and began reading the prayers, making the sign of the cross and prostrating himself. 'Can it be that this couch will be my bier?' he read. And it seemed as if a devil whispered to him: 'A solitary couch is itself a bier. Falsehood!' And in imagination he saw the shoulders of a widow with whom he had lived. He shook himself, and went on reading. Having read the precepts he took up the Gospels, opened the book, and happened on a passage he often repeated and knew by heart: 'Lord, I believe. Help thou my unbelief!'—and he put away all the doubts that had arisen. As one replaces an object of insecure equilibrium, so he carefully replaced his belief on its shaky pedestal and carefully stepped back from it so as not to shake or upset it. The blinkers were adjusted again and he felt tranquil, and repeating his childhood's prayer: 'Lord, receive me, receive me!' He felt not merely at ease, but thrilled and joyful. He crossed himself and lay down on the bedding on his narrow bench, tucking his summer cassock under his head. He fell asleep at once, and in his light slumber he seemed to hear the tinkling of sledge bells. He did not know whether he was dreaming or awake, but a knock at the door aroused him. He sat up, distrusting his senses, but the knock was repeated. Yes, it was a knock close at hand, at his door, and with it the sound of a woman's voice.

'My God! Can it be true, as I have read in the *Lives of the Saints*, that the devil takes on the form of a woman? Yes—it is a woman's voice. And a tender, timid, pleasant voice. Phew!' And he spat to exorcise the devil. 'No, it was only my imagination,' he assured himself, and he went to the corner where his lectern stood, falling on his knees in the regular and habitual manner which of itself gave him consolation and satisfaction. He sank down, his hair hanging over his face, and pressed his head, already going bald in front, to the cold damp strip of drugget on the draughty floor. He read the psalm old Father Pimen had told him warded off temptation. He easily raised his light and emaciated body on his strong sinewy legs and tried to continue saying his prayers, but instead of doing so he involuntarily strained his hearing. He wished to hear more. All was quiet.

From the corner of the roof regular drops continued to fall into the tub below. Outside was a mist and fog eating into the snow that lay on the ground. It was still, very still. And suddenly there was a rustling at the window and a voice—that same tender, timid voice, which could only belong to an attractive woman—said:

'Let me in, for the sake of Christ!'

It seemed as though his blood had all rushed to his heart and settled there. He could hardly breathe. 'Let God arise and let his enemies be scattered...'

'But I am not a devil!' It was obvious that the lips that uttered this were smiling. 'I am not a devil, but only a sinful woman who has lost her way, not figuratively but literally!' She laughed. 'I am frozen and beg for shelter.'

He pressed his face to the window, but the little icon-lamp was reflected by it and shone on the whole pane. He put his hands to both sides of his face and peered between them. Fog, mist, a tree, and—just opposite him—she herself. Yes, there, a few inches from him, was the sweet, kindly frightened face of a woman in a cap and a coat of long white fur, leaning towards him. Their eyes met with instant recognition: not that they had ever known one another, they had never met before, but by the look they exchanged they—and he particularly—felt that they knew and understood one another. After that glance to imagine her to be a devil and not a simple, kindly, sweet, timid woman, was impossible.

'Who are you? Why have you come?' he asked.

'Do please open the door!' she replied, with capricious authority. 'I am frozen. I tell you I have lost my way.'

'But I am a monk—a hermit.'

'Oh, do please open the door—or do you wish me to freeze under your window while you say your prayers?'

'But how have you...'

'I shan't eat you. For God's sake let me in! I am quite frozen.'

She really did feel afraid, and said this in an almost tearful voice.

He stepped back from the window and looked at an icon of the Saviour in His crown of thorns. 'Lord, help me! Lord, help me!' he exclaimed, crossing himself and bowing low. Then he went to the door, and opening it into the tiny porch, felt for the hook that fastened the outer door and began to lift it. He heard steps outside. She was coming from the window to the door. 'Ah!' she suddenly exclaimed, and he understood that she had stepped into the puddle that the dripping from the roof had formed at the threshold. His hands trembled, and could not raise the hook of the tightly closed door.

'Oh, what are you doing? Let me in! I am all wet. I am frozen! You are thinking about saving your soul and are letting me freeze to death . . .'

He jerked the door towards him, raised the hook, and without considering what he was doing, pushed it open with such force that it struck her.

'Oh— *pardon!*' he suddenly exclaimed, reverting completely to his old manner with ladies.

She smiled on hearing that *pardon*. 'He is not quite so terrible, after all,' she thought. 'It's all right. It is you who must pardon me,' she said, stepping past him. 'I should never have ventured, but such an extraordinary circumstance . . .'

'If you please!' he uttered, and stood aside to let her pass him. A strong smell of fine scent, which he had long not encountered, assailed him. She went through the little porch into the cell where he lived. He closed the outer door without fastening the hook, and stepped in after her.

'Lord Jesus Christ, Son of God, have mercy on me a sinner! Lord, have mercy on me a sinner!' he prayed unceasingly, not merely to himself but involuntarily moving his lips. 'If you please!' he said to her again. She stood in the middle of the room, moisture dripping from her to the floor as she looked him over. Her eyes were laughing.

'Forgive me for having disturbed your solitude. But you see what a position I am in. It all came about from our starting from town for a sledge-drive, and my making a bet that I would walk back by myself from the Vorobevka to the town. But then I lost my way, and if I had not happened to come upon you cell...' She began lying, but became silent. She had not expected him to be at all such as he was. He was not as handsome as she had imagined, but was nevertheless beautiful in her eyes: his greyish hair and beard, slightly curling, his fine, regular nose, and his eyes like glowing coal when he looked at her, made a strong impression on her.

He saw that she was lying.

'Yes... so,' said he, looking at her and again lowering his eyes. 'I will go in there, and this place is at your disposal.'

And taking down the little lamp, he lit a candle, and bowing low to her went into a small cell beyond the partition, and she heard him begin to move something about there. 'Probably he is barricading himself in from me!' she though with a smile, and throwing off her white dogskin cloak she tried to take off her cap, which had become entangled in her hair and in the woven kerchief she was wearing under it. She had not got all wet when standing under the window, and had said so only as a pretext to get him to let her in. But she really had stepped into the puddle at the door, and her left foot was wet up to the ankle and her overshoe full of water. She sat down on his bed—a bench only covered by a piece of carpet—and began to take off her boots. The little cell seemed to her charming. The narrow little room, some seven feet by nine, was a clean as glass. There was nothing in it but the bench on which she was sitting, the book-shelf above it, and a lectern in the corner. A sheepskin coat and a cassock hung on nails by the door. Above the lectern was the little lamp and an icon of Christ in His crown of thorns. The room smelt strangely of perspiration and of earth. It all pleased her—even that smell. Her wet feet, especially one of them, were uncomfortable, and she quickly began to take off her boots and stockings without ceasing to smile, pleased not so much at having achieved her object as because she perceived that she had abashed that charming, strange, striking, and attractive man. 'He did not respond, but what of that?' she said to herself.

'Father Sergius! Father Sergius! Or how does one call you?'

'What do you want?' replied a quiet voice.

'Please forgive me for disturbing your solitude, but really I could not help it. I should simply have fallen ill. And I don't know that I shan't now. I am all wet and my feet are like ice.'

'Pardon me,' replied the quiet voice. 'I cannot be of any assistance to you.'

'I would not have disturbed you if I could have helped it. I am only here till daybreak.'

He did not reply and she heard him muttering something, probably his prayers.

'You will not be coming in here?' she asked, smiling. 'For I must undress to dry myself.'

He did not reply, but continued to read his prayers.

'Yes, that is a man!' thought she, getting her dripping boot off with difficulty. She tugged at it, but could not get it off. The absurdity of it struck her and she began to laugh almost inaudibly. But knowing that he would hear her laughter and would be moved by it just as she wished him to be, she laughed louder, and her laughter—gay, natural, and kindly—really acted on him just in the way she wished.

'Yes, I could love a man like that—such eyes and such a simple noble face, and passionate too despite all the prayers he mutters!' thought she. 'You can't deceive a woman in these things. As soon as he put his face to the window and saw me, he understood and knew. The glimmer of it was in his eyes and remained there. He began to love me and desired me. Yes—desired!' said she, getting her overshoe and her boot off at last and starting to take off her stockings. To remove those long stockings fastened with elastic it

was necessary to raise her skirts. She felt embarrassed and said:
'Don't come in!'

But there was no reply from the other side of the well. The steady muttering continued and also a sound of moving.

'He is prostrating himself to the ground, no doubt,' thought she. 'But he won't bow himself out of it. He is thinking of me just as I am thinking of him. He is thinking of these feet of mine with the same feeling that I have!' And she pulled off her wet stockings and put her feet up on the bench, pressing them under her. She sat a while like that with her arms round her knees and looking pensively before her. 'But it is a desert, here in this silence. No one would ever know. . . .'

She rose, took her stockings over to the stove, and hung them on the damper. It was a queer damper, and she turned it about, and then, stepping lightly on her bare feet, returned to the bench and sat down there again with her feet up.

There was complete silence on the other side of the partition. She looked at the tiny watch that hung round her neck. It was two o'clock. 'Our party should return about three!' She had not more than an hour before her. 'Well, am I to sit like this all alone? What nonsense! I don't want to. I will call him at once.'

'Father Sergius, Father Sergius! Sergey Dmitrich! Prince Kasatsky!'

Beyond the partition all was silent.

'Listen! This is cruel. I would not call you if it were not necessary. I am ill. I don't know what is the matter with me!' she exclaimed in a tone of suffering. 'Oh! Oh!' she groaned, falling back on the bench. And strange to say she really felt that her strength was failing, that she was becoming faint, that everything in her ached, and that she was shivering with fever.

'Listen! Help me! I don't know what is the matter with me. Oh! Oh!' She unfastened her dress, exposing her breast, and lifted her arms, bare to the elbow. 'Oh! Oh!'

All this time he stood on the other side of the partition and prayed. Having finished all the evening prayers, he now stood motionless, his eyes looking at the end of his nose, and mentally repeated with all his soul: 'Lord Jesus Christ, Son of God, have mercy upon me!'

But he had heard everything. He had heard how the silk rustled when she took off her dress, how she stepped with bare feet on the floor, and had heard how she rubbed her feet with her hand. He felt his own weakness, and that he might be lost at any moment. That was why he prayed unceasingly. He felt rather as the hero in the fairy-tale must have felt when he had to go on and on without looking round. So Sergius heard and felt that danger and destruction were there, hovering above and around him, and that he could only save himself by not looking in that direction for an instant. But suddenly the desire to look seized him. At the same instant she said:

'This is inhuman. I may die. . . .'

'Yes, I will go to her, but like the Saint who laid one hand on the adulteress and thrust his other into the brazier. But there is no brazier here.' He looked round. The lamp! He put his finger over the flame and frowned, preparing himself to suffer. And for a rather long time, as it seemed to him, there was no sensation, but suddenly—he had not yet decided whether it was painful enough—he writhed all over, jerked his hand away, and waved it in the air. 'No, I can't stand that!'

'For God's sake come to me! I am dying! Oh!'

'Well—shall I perish? No, not so!'

'I will come to you directly,' he said, and having opened his door, he went without looking at her through the cell into the porch where he used to chop wood. There he felt for the block and for an axe which leant against the wall.

'Immediately!' he said, and taking up the axe with his right hand he laid the forefinger of his left hand on the block, swung the axe, and struck with it below the second joint. The finger flew off more lightly than a stick of similar thickness, and jumping up, dropped over on the edge of the block and then fell to the floor.

He heard it fall before he felt any pain, but before he had time to be surprised he felt a burning pain and the warmth of flowing blood. He hastily wrapped the stump in the skirt of his cassock, and pressing it to his hip went back into the room, and standing in front of the woman, lowered his eyes and asked in a low voice: 'What do you want?'

She looked at his pale face and his quivering left cheek, and suddenly felt ashamed. She jumped up, seized her furcloak, and throwing it round her shoulders, wrapped herself up in it.

'I was in pain . . . I have caught cold . . . I . . . Father Sergius . . . I …'

He let his eyes, shining with a quiet light of joy, rest upon her, and said:

'Dear sister, why did you wish to ruin your immortal soul? Temptations must come into the world, but woe to him by whom temptation comes. Pray that God may forgive us!'

She listened and looked at him. Suddenly she heard the sound of something dripping. She looked down and saw that blood was flowing from his hand and down his cassock.

'What have you done to your hand?' She remembered the sound she had heard, and seizing the little lamp ran out into the porch. There on the floor she saw the bloody finger. She returned with her face paler than his and was about to speak to him, but he silently passed into the back cell and fastened the door.

'Forgive me!' she said. 'How can I atone for my sin?'

'Go away.'

'Let me tie up your hand.'

'Go away from here.'

She dressed hurriedly and silently, and when ready sat waiting in her furs. The sledge-bells were heard outside.

'Father Sergius, forgive me!'

'Go away. God will forgive.'

'Father Sergius! I will change my life. Do not forsake me!'

'Go away.'

'Forgive me—and give me your blessing!'

'In the name of the Father and of the Son and of the Holy Ghost!'—she heard his voice from behind the partition. 'Go!'

She burst into sobs and left the cell. The lawyer came forward to meet her.

'Well, I see I have lost the bet. It can't be helped. Where will you sit?'

'It is all the same to me.'

She took a seat in the sledge, and did not utter a word all the way home.

A year later she entered a convent as a novice, and lived a strict life under the direction of the hermit Arseny, who wrote letters to her at long intervals.

IV

Father Sergius lived as a recluse for another seven years.

At first he accepted much of what people brought him—tea, sugar, white bread, milk, clothing, and firewood. But as time went on he led a more and more and more austere life, refusing everything superfluous, and finally he accepted nothing but rye-bread once a week. Everything else that was brought him he gave to the poor who came to him. He spent his entire time in his cell, in prayer or in conversation with callers, who became more and more numerous as time went on. Only three times a year did he go out to church, and when necessary he went out to fetch water and wood.

The episode with Makovkina had occurred after five years of his hermit life. That occurrence soon became generally known—her nocturnal visit, the change she underwent, and her entry into a convent. From that time Father Sergius's fame increased. More and more visitors came to see him, other monks settled down near his cell, and a church was erected there and also a hostelry. His fame, as usual exaggerating his feats, spread ever more and more widely. People began to come to him from a distance, and began bringing invalids to him whom they declared he cured.

His first cure occurred in the eighth year of his life as a hermit. It was the healing of a fourteen-year-old boy, whose mother brought him to Father Sergius insisting that he should lay his hand on the child's head. It had never occurred to Father Sergius that he could cure the sick. He would have regarded such a thought as a great sin of pride; but the mother who brought the boy implored him insistently, falling at his feet and saying: 'Why do you, who heal others, refuse to help my son?' She besought him in Christ's name. When Father Sergius assured her that only God could heal the sick, she replied that she only wanted him to lay his hands on the boy and pray for him. Father Sergius refused and returned to his cell. But next day (it was in autumn and the nights were already cold) on going out for water he saw the same mother with her son, a pale youngster of fourteen, and was met by the same petition.

He remembered the parable of the unjust judge, and though he had previously felt sure that he ought to refuse, he now began to hesitate and, having hesitated, took to prayer and prayed until a decision formed itself in his soul. This decision was that he ought to accede to the woman's request and that her faith might save her son. As for himself, he would in the case be but an insignificant instrument chosen by God.

And going out to the mother he did what she asked—laid his hand on the boy's head and prayed.

The mother left with her son, and a month later the boy recovered, and the fame of the holy healing power of the *stárets* Sergius (as they now called him) spread throughout the whole district. After that, not a week passed without sick people coming, riding or on foot, to Father Sergius; and having acceded to one petition he could not refuse others, and he laid his hands on many and prayed. Many recovered, and his fame spread more and more.

So seven years passed in the Monastery and thirteen in his hermit's cell. He now had the appearance of an old man: his beard was long and grey, but his hair, though thin, was still black and curly.

V

For some weeks Father Sergius had been living with one persistent thought: whether he was right in accepting the position in which he had not so much placed himself as been placed by the Archimandrite and the Abbot. That position had begun after the recovery of the fourteen-year-old boy. From that time, with each month, week, and day that passed, Sergius felt his own inner life wasting away and being replaced by external life. It was as if he had been turned inside out.

Sergius saw that he was a means of attracting visitors and contributions to the monastery, and that therefore the authorities arranged matters in such a way as to make as much use of him as possible. For instance, they rendered it impossible for him to do any manual work. He was supplied with everything he could want, and they demanded of him only that he should not refuse his blessing to those who came to seek it. For his convenience they appointed days when he would receive. They arranged a reception-room for men, and a place was railed in so that he should not be pushed over by the crowds of women visitors, and so that he could conveniently bless those who came.

They told him that people needed him, and that fulfilling Christ's law of love he could not refuse their demand to see him, and that to avoid them would be cruel. He could not but agree with this, but the more he gave himself up to such a life the more he felt that what was internal became external, and that the fount of living water within him dried up, and that what he did now was done more and more for men and less and less for God.

Whether he admonished people, or simply blessed them, or prayed for the sick, or advised people about their lives, or listened to expressions of gratitude from those he had helped by precepts, or alms, or healing (as they assured him)—he could not help being pleased at it, and could not be indifferent to the results of his activity and to the influence he exerted. He thought himself a shining light, and the more he felt this the more was he conscious of a weakening, a dying down of the divine light of truth that shone within him.

'In how far is what I do for God and in how far is it for men?' That was the question that insistently tormented him and to which he was not so much unable to give himself an answer as unable to face the answer.

In the depth of his soul he felt that the devil had substituted an activity for men in place of his former activity for God. He felt this because, just as it had formerly been hard for him to be torn from his solitude so now that solitude itself was hard for him. He was oppressed and wearied by visitors, but at the bottom of his heart he was glad of their presence and glad of the praise they heaped upon him.

There was a time when he decided to go away and hide. He even planned all that was necessary for that purpose. He prepared for himself a peasant's shirt, trousers, coat, and cap. He explained that he wanted these to give to those who asked. He kept these clothes in his cell, planning how he would put them on, cut his hair short, and go away. First he would go some three hundred versts by train, then he would leave the train and walk from village to village. He asked an old man who had been a soldier how he tramped: what people gave him, and what shelter they allowed him. The soldier told him where people were most charitable, and where they would take a wanderer in for the night, and Father Sergius intended to avail himself of this information. He even put on those clothes one night in his desire to go, but he could not decide what was best—to remain or to escape. At first he was in doubt, but afterwards this indecision passed. He submitted to custom and yielded to the devil, and only the peasant garb reminded him of the thought and feeling he had had.

Every day more and more people flocked to him and less and less time was left him for prayer and for renewing his spiritual strength. Sometimes in lucid moments he thought he was like a place where there had once been a spring. 'There used to be a feeble spring of living water which flowed quietly from me and through me. That was true life, the time when she tempted me!' (He always thought with ecstasy of that night and of her who was now Mother Agnes.) She had tasted of that pure water, but since then there had not been time for it to collect before thirsty people came crowding in and pushing one another aside. And they had trampled everything down and nothing was left but mud.

So he thought in rare moments of lucidity, but his usual state of mind was one of weariness and a tender pity for himself because of that weariness.

It was in spring, on the eve of the mid-Pentecostal feast. Father Sergius was officiating at the Vigil Service in his hermitage church, where the congregation was as large as the little church could hold—about twenty people. They were all well-to-do proprietors or merchants. Father Sergius admitted anyone, but a selection was made by the monk in attendance and by an assistant who was sent to the hermitage every day from the monastery. A crowd of some eighty people—pilgrims and peasants, and especially peasant-women—stood outside waiting for Father Sergius to come out and bless them. Meanwhile he conducted the service, but at the point at which he went out to the tomb of his predecessor, he staggered and would have fallen had he not been caught by a merchant standing behind him and by the monk acting as deacon.

'What is the matter, Father Sergius? Dear man! O Lord!' exclaimed the women. 'He is as white as a sheet!'

But Father Sergius recovered immediately, and though very pale, he waved the merchant and the deacon aside and continued to chant the service.

Father Seraphim, the deacon, the acolytes, and Sofya Ivanovna, a lady who always lived near the hermitage and tended Father Sergius, begged him to bring the service to an end.

'No, there's nothing the matter,' said Father Sergius, slightly smiling from beneath his moustache and continuing the service. 'Yes, that is the way the Saints behaved!' thought he.

'A holy man—an angel of God!' he heard just then the voice of Sofya Ivanovna behind him, and also of the merchant who had supported him. He did not heed their entreaties, but went on with the service. Again crowding together they all made their way by the narrow passages back into the little church, and there, though abbreviating it slightly, Father Sergius completed vespers.

Immediately after the service Father Sergius, having pronounced the benediction on those present, went over to the bench under the elm tree at the entrance to the cave. He wished to rest and breathe the fresh air—he felt in need of it. But as soon as he left the church the crowd of people rushed to him soliciting his blessing, his advice, and his help. There were pilgrims who constantly tramped from one holy place to another and from one *stárets* to another, and were always entranced by every shrine and every *stárets*. Father Sergius knew this common, cold, conventional, and most irreligious type. There were pilgrims, for the most part discharged soldiers, unaccustomed to a settled life, poverty-stricken, and many of them drunken old men, who tramped from monastery to monastery merely to be fed. And there were rough peasants and peasant-women who had come with their selfish requirements, seeking cures or to have doubts about quite practical affairs solved for them: about marrying off a daughter, or hiring a shop, or buying a bit of land, or how to atone for having overlaid a child of having an illegitimate one.

All this was an old story and not in the least interesting to him. He knew he would hear nothing new from these folk, that they would arouse no religious emotion in him; but he liked to see the crowd to which his blessing and advice was necessary and precious, so while that crowd oppressed him it also pleased him. Father Seraphim began to drive them away, saying that Father Sergius was tired. But Father Sergius, remembering the words of Jesus in the Gospel, referring to children: 'Forbid them not to come unto me', and feeling tenderly towards himself at this recollection, said they should be allowed to approach.

He rose, went to the railing beyond which the crowd had gathered, and began blessing them and answering their questions, but in a voice so weak that he was touched with pity for himself. Yet despite his wish to receive them all he could not do it. Things again grew dark before his eyes, and he staggered and grasped the railings. He felt a rush of blood to his head and first went pale and then suddenly flushed.

'I must leave the rest till tomorrow. I cannot do more today,' he murmured, and, pronouncing a general benediction, returned to the bench. The merchant again supported him, and leading him by the arm helped him to be seated.

'Father!' came voices from the crowd. 'Dear Father! Do not forsake us. Without you we are lost!'

The merchant, having seated Father Sergius on the bench under the elm, took on himself police duties and drove the people off very resolutely. It is true that he spoke in a low voice so that Father Sergius might not hear him, but his words were incisive and angry.

'Be off, be off! He has blessed you, and what more do you want? Get along with you, or I'll wring your necks! Move on there! Get along, you old woman with your dirty leg-bands! Go, go! Where are you shoving to? You've been told that it is finished. Tomorrow will be as God wills, but for today he has finished!'

'Father! Only let my eyes have a glimpse of his dear face!' said an old woman.

'I'll glimpse you! Where are you shoving to?'

Father Sergius noticed that the merchant seemed to be acting roughly, and in a feeble voice told the attendant that the people should not be driven away. He knew that they would be driven away all the same, and he much desired to be left alone and to rest, but he sent the attendant with that message to produce an impression.

'All right, all right! I am not driving them away. I am only remonstrating with them,' replied the merchant. 'You know they wouldn't hesitate to drive a man to death. They have no pity, they only consider themselves. . . . ; You've been told you cannot see him. Go away! Tomorrow!' And he got rid of them all.

He took all these pains because he liked order and liked to domineer and drive the people away, but chiefly because he wanted to have Father Sergius to himself. He was a widower with an only daughter who was an invalid and unmarried, and whom he had brought fourteen hundred versts to Father Sergius to be healed. For two years past he had been taking her to different places to be cured: first to the university clinic in the chief town of the province, but that did no good; then to a peasant in the province of Samara, where she got a little better; then to a doctor in Moscow to whom he paid much money, but this did no good at all. Now he had been told that Father Sergius wrought cures, and had brought her to him. So when all the people had been driven away he approached Father Sergius, and suddenly falling on his knees loudly exclaimed:

'Holy Father! Bless my afflicted offspring that she may be healed of her malady. I venture to prostrate myself at your holy feet.'

And he placed one hand in the other, cup-wise. He said and did all this as if he were doing something clearly and firmly appointed by law and usage—as if one must and should ask for a daughter to be cured in just this way and no other. He did it with such conviction that it seemed even to Father Sergius that it should be said and done in just that way, but nevertheless he bade him rise and tell him what the trouble was. The merchant said that his daughter, a girl of twenty-two, had fallen ill two years ago, after her mother's sudden death. She had moaned (as he expressed it) and since then had not been herself. And now he had brought her fourteen hundred versts and she was waiting in the hostelry till Father Sergius should give orders to bring her. She did not go out during the day, being afraid of the light, and could only come after sunset.

'Is she very weak?' asked Father Sergius.

'No, she has no particular weakness. She is quite plump, and is only "neurasthenic" the doctors say. If you will only let me bring her this evening, Father Sergius, I'll fly like a spirit to fetch her. Holy Father! Revive a parent's heart, restore his line, save his afflicted daughter by your prayers!' And the merchant again threw himself on his knees and bending sideways, with his head resting on his clenched fists, remained stock still. Father Sergius again told him to get up, and thinking how burdensome his activities were and even so how patiently he carried through with them, he sighed heavily and after a few seconds of silence, said:

'Well, bring her this evening, I will pray for her, but now I am tired . . . ;' and he closed his eyes. 'I will send for you.'

The merchant went away, stepping on tiptoe, which only made his boots creak the louder, and Father Sergius remained alone.

His whole life was filled by church services and by people who came to see him, but today had been a particularly difficult one. In the morning an important official had arrived and had had a long conversation with him; after that a lady had come with her son. This son was a sceptical young professor whom the mother, an ardent believer and devoted to Father Sergius, had brought that he might talk to him. The conversation had been very trying.

The young man, evidently not wishing to have a controversy with a monk, had agreed with him in everything as with someone who was mentally inferior. Father Sergius saw that the young man did not believe but yet was content with himself, tranquil, and at ease, and the memory of that conversation now disquieted him.

'Have something to eat, Father,' said the attendant.

'All right, bring me something.'

The attendant went to a hut that had been arranged some ten paces from the cave, and Father Sergius remained alone.

The time was long past when he had lived alone, doing everything for himself and eating only rye-bread, or rolls prepared for the church. He had been advised long since that he had no right to neglect his health, and he was given wholesome, though Lenten, food. He ate sparingly, though much more than he had done, and often he ate with much pleasure, and not as formerly with aversion and a sense of guilt. So it was now. He had some gruel, drank a cup of tea, and ate half a white roll.

The attendant went away, and Father Sergius remained alone under the elm tree.

It was a wonderful May evening, when the birches, aspens, elms, wild cherries, and oaks, had just burst into foliage.

The bush of wild cherries behind the elm tree was in full bloom and had not yet begun to shed its blossoms, and the nightingales—one quite near at hand and two or three others in the bushes down by the river—burst into full song after some preliminary twittering. From the river came the far-off songs of peasants returning, no doubt, from their work. The sun was setting behind the forest, its last rays glowing through the leaves. All that side was brilliant green, the other side with the elm tree was dark. Cockchafers flew clumsily about, falling to the ground when they collided with anything.

After supper Father Sergius began to repeat a silent prayer: 'O Lord Jesus Christ, Son of God, have mercy upon us!' and then he read a psalm, and suddenly in the middle of the psalm a sparrow flew out from the bush, alighted on the ground, and hopped towards him chirping as it came, but then it took fright at something and flew away. He said a prayer which referred to his abandonment of the world, and hastened to finish it in order to send for the merchant with the sick daughter. She interested him in that she presented a distraction, and because both she and her father considered him a saint whose prayers were efficacious. Outwardly he disavowed that idea, but in the depths of his soul he considered it to be true.

He was often amazed that this had happened, that he, Stepan Kasatsky, had come to be such an extraordinary saint and even a worker of miracles; but of the fact that he was such there could not be the least doubt. He could not fail to believe in the miracles he himself witnessed, beginning with the sick boy and ending with the old woman who had recovered her sight when he had prayed for her.

Strange as it might be, it was so. Accordingly the merchant's daughter interested him as a new individual who had faith in him, and also as a fresh opportunity to confirm his healing powers and enhance his fame. 'They bring people a thousand versts and write about it in the papers. The Emperor knows of it, and they know of it in Europe, in unbelieving Europe'—thought he. And suddenly he felt ashamed of his vanity and again began to pray. 'Lord, King of Heaven, Comforter, Soul of Truth! Come and enter into me and cleanse me from all sin and save and bless my soul. Cleanse me from the sin of worldly vanity that troubles me!' he repeated, and he remembered how often he had prayed about this and how vain till now his prayers had been in that respect. His prayers worked miracles for others, but in his own case God had not granted him liberation from this petty passion.

He remembered his prayers at the commencement of his life at the hermitage, when he prayed for purity, humility, and love, and how it seemed to him then that God heard his prayers. He had retained his purity and had chopped off his finger. And he lifted the shrivelled stump of that finger to his lips and kissed it. It seemed to him now that he had been humble then when he had always seemed loathsome to himself on account of his sinfulness; and when he remembered the tender feelings with which he had then met an old man who was bringing a drunken soldier to him to ask alms. When he had received *her*, it seemed to him that he had then possessed love also. But now? And he asked himself whether he loved anyone, whether he loved Sofya Ivanovna, or Father Seraphim, whether he had any feeling of love for all who had come to him that day—for that learned young man with whom he had had that instructive discussion in which he was concerned only to show off his own intelligence and that he had not lagged behind the times in knowledge. He wanted and needed their love, but felt none towards them. He now had neither love nor humility nor purity.

He was pleased to know that the merchant's daughter was twenty-two, and he wondered whether she was goodlooking. When he inquired whether she was weak, he really wanted to know if she had feminine charm.

'Can I have fallen so low?' he thought. 'Lord, help me! Restore me, my Lord and God!' And he clasped his hands and began to pray.

The nightingales burst into song, a cockchafer knocked against him and crept up the back of his neck. He brushed it off. 'But does He exist? What if I am knocking at a door fastened from outside? The bar is on the door for all to see. Nature—the nightingales and the cockchafers—is that bar. Perhaps the young man was right.' And he began to pray aloud. He prayed for a long time till these thoughts vanished and he again felt calm and confident. He rang the bell and told the attendant to say that the merchant might bring his daughter to him now.

The merchant came, leading his daughter by the arm. He led her into the cell and immediately left her.

She was a very fair girl, plump and very short, with a pale, frightened, childish face and a fully developed feminine figure. Father Sergius remained seated on the bench at the entrance and when she was passing and stopped beside him for his blessing he was aghast at himself for the way he looked at her figure. As she passed by him he was acutely conscious of her femininity, though he saw by her face that she was sensual and feeble-minded. He rose and went into the cell. She was sitting on a stool waiting for him, and when he entered she rose.

'I want to go back to Papa,' she said.

'Don't be afraid,' he replied. 'What are you suffering from?'

'I am in pain all over,' she said, and suddenly her face lit up with a smile.

'You will be well,' said he. 'Pray!'

'What is the use of praying? I have prayed and it does no good'—and she continued to smile. 'I want you to pray for me and lay your hands on me. I saw you in a dream.'

'How did you see me?'

'I saw you put your hands on my breast like that.' She took his hand and pressed it to her breast. 'Just here.'

He yielded his right hand to her.

'What is your name?' he asked, trembling all over and feeling that he was overcome and that his desire had already passed beyond control.

'Marie. Why?'

She took his hand and kissed it, and then put her arm round his waist and pressed him to herself.

'What are you doing?' he said. 'Marie, you are a devil!'

'Oh, perhaps. What does it matter?'

And embracing him she sat down with him on the bed.

At dawn he went out into the porch.

'Can this all have happened? Her father will come and she will tell him everything. She is a devil! What am I to do? Here is the axe with which I chopped off my finger.' He snatched up the axe and moved back towards the cell.

The attendant came up.

'Do you want some wood chopped? Let me have the axe.'

Sergius yielded up the axe and entered the cell. She was lying there asleep. He looked at her with horror, and passed on beyond the partition, where he took down the peasant clothes and put them on. Then he seized a pair of scissors, cut off his long hair, and went out along the path down the hill to the river, where he had not been for more than three years.

A road ran beside the river and he went along it and walked till noon. Then he went into a field of rye and lay down there. Towards evening he approached a village, but without entering it went towards the cliff that overhung the river. There he again lay down to rest.

It was early morning, half an hour before sunrise. All was damp and gloomy and a cold early wind was blowing from the west. 'Yes, I must end it all. There is no God. But how am I to end it? Throw myself into the river? I can swim and should not drown. Hang myself? Yes, just throw this sash over a branch.' This seemed so feasible and so easy that he felt horrified. As usual at moments of despair he felt the need of prayer. But there was no one to pray to. There was no God. He lay down resting on his arm, and suddenly such a longing for sleep overcame him that he could no longer support his head on his hand, but stretched out his arm, laid his head upon it, and fell asleep. But that sleep lasted only for a moment. He woke up immediately and began not to dream but to remember.

He saw himself as a child in his mother's home in the country. A carriage drives up, and out of it steps Uncle Nicholas Sergeivich, with his long, spade-shaped, black beard, and with him Pashenka, a thin little girl with large mild eyes and a timid pathetic face. And into their company of boys Pashenka is brought and they have to play with her, but it is dull. She is silly, and it ends by their making fun of her and forcing her to show

how she can swim. She lies down on the floor and shows them, and they all laugh and make a fool of her. She sees this and blushes red in patches and becomes more pitiable than before, so pitiable that he feels ashamed and can never forget that crooked, kindly, submissive smile. And Sergius remembered having seen her since then. Long after, just before he became a monk, she had married a landowner who squandered all her fortune and was in the habit of beating her. She had had two children, a son and a daughter, but the son had died while still young. And Sergius remembered having seen her very wretched. Then again he had seen her in the monastery when she was a widow. She had been still the same, not exactly stupid, but insipid, insignificant, and pitiable. She had come with her daughter and her daughter's fiancé. They were already poor at that time and later on he had heard that she was living in a small provincial town and was very hard up.

'Why am I thinking about her?' He asked himself, but he could not cease doing so. 'Where is she? How is she getting on? Is she still as unhappy as she was then when she had to show us how to swim on the floor? But why should I think about her? What am I doing? I must put an end to myself.'

And again he felt afraid, and again, to escape from that thought, he went on thinking about Pashenka.

So he lay for a long time, thinking now of his unavoidable end and now of Pashenka. She presented herself to him as a means of salvation. At last he fell asleep, and in his sleep he saw an angel who came to him and said: 'Go to Pashenka and learn from her what you have to do, what your sin is, and wherein lies your salvation.'

He awoke, and having decided that this was a vision sent by God, he felt glad, and resolved to do what had been told him in the vision. He knew the town where she lived. It was some three hundred versts [two hundred miles] away, and he set out to walk there.

VI

Pashenka had already long ceased to be Pashenka and had become old, withered, wrinkled Praskovya Mikhaylovna, mother-in-law of that failure, the drunken official Mavrikyev. She was living in the country town where he had had his last appointment, and there she was supporting the family: her daughter, her ailing neurasthenic son-in-law, and her five grandchildren. She did this by giving music lessons to tradesmen's daughters, giving four and sometimes five lessons a day of an hour each, and earning in this way some sixty roubles—a pittance—a month. So they lived for the present, in expectation of another appointment. She had sent letters to all her relations and acquaintances asking them to obtain a post for her son-in-law, and among the rest she had written to Sergius, but that letter had not reached him.

It was a Saturday, and Praskovya Mikhaylovna was herself mixing dough for currant bread such as the serf-cook on her father's estate used to make so well. She wished to give her grandchildren a treat on the Sunday.

Masha, her daughter, was nursing her youngest child, the eldest boy and girl were at school, and her son-in-law was asleep, not having slept during the night. Praskovya Mikhaylovna had remained awake too for a great part of the night, trying to soften her daughter's anger against her husband.

She saw that it was impossible for her son-in-law, a weak creature, to be other than he was, and realized that his wife's reproaches could do no good—so she used all her efforts to allay those reproaches and to avoid recrimination and anger. Unkindly relations between people caused her actual physical suffering. It was so clear to her that bitter feelings do not make anything better, but only make everything worse. She did not in fact think about this: she simply suffered at the sight of anger as she would from a bad smell, a harsh noise, or from blows on her body.

She had—with a feeling of self-satisfaction—just taught Lukerya how to mix the dough, when her six-year-old grandson Misha, wearing an apron and with darned stockings on his crooked little legs, ran into the kitchen with a frightened face.

'Grandma, a dreadful old man wants to see you.'

Lukerya looked out at the door.

'There is a pilgrim of some kind, a man . . .'

Praskovya Mikhaylovna rubbed her thin elbows against one another, wiped her hands on her apron and went upstairs to get a five-kopek piece out of her purse for him, but remembering that she had nothing less than a ten-kopek piece she decided to give him some bread instead. She returned to the cupboard, but suddenly blushed at the thought of having grudged the ten-kopek piece, and telling Lukerya to cut a slice of bread, went upstairs again to fetch it. 'It serves you right,' she said to herself. 'You must now give twice over.'

She gave both the bread and the money to the pilgrim, and when doing so—far from being proud of her generosity—she excused herself for giving so little. The man had such an imposing appearance.

Though he had tramped two hundred versts as a beggar, though he was tattered and had grown thin and weather-beaten, though he had cropped his long hair and was wearing a peasant's cap and boots, and though he bowed very humbly, Sergius still had the impressive appearance that made him so attractive. But Praskovya Mikhaylovna did not recognize him. She could hardly do so, not having seen him for almost twenty years.

'Don't think ill of me, Father. Perhaps you want something to eat?'

He took the bread and the money, and Praskovya Mikhaylovna was surprised that he did not go, but stood looking at her.

'Pashenka, I have come to you! Take me in . . .'

His beautiful black eyes, shining with the tears that started in them, were fixed on her with imploring insistence. And under his greyish moustache his lips quivered piteously.

Praskovya Mikhaylovna pressed her hands to her withered breast, opened her mouth, and stood petrified, staring at the pilgrim with dilated eyes.

'It can't be! Stepa! Sergey! Father Sergius!'

'Yes, it is I,' said Sergius in a low voice. 'Only not Sergius, or Father Sergius, but a great sinner, Stepan Kasatsky—a great and lost sinner. Take me in and help me!'

'It's impossible! How have you so humbled yourself? But come in.'

She reached out her hand, but he did not take it and only followed her in.

But where was she to take him? The lodging was a small one. Formerly she had had a tiny room, almost a closet, for herself, but later she had given it up to her daughter, and Masha was now sitting there rocking the baby.

'Sit here for the present,' she said to Sergius, pointing to a bench in the kitchen.

He sat down at once, and with an evidently accustomed movement slipped the straps of his wallet first off one shoulder and then off the other.

'My God, my God! How you have humbled yourself, Father! Such great fame, and now like this . . .'

Sergius did not reply, but only smiled meekly, placing his wallet under the bench on which he sat.

'Masha, do you know who this is?'—And in a whisper Praskovya Mikhaylovna told her daughter who he was, and together they then carried the bed and the cradle out of the tiny room and cleared it for Sergius.

Praskovya Mikhaylovna led him into it.

'Here you can rest. Don't take offence . . . but I must go out.'

'Where to?'

'I have to go to a lesson, I am ashamed to tell you, but I teach music!'

'Music? But that is good. Only just one thing, Praskovya Mikhaylovna, I have come to you with a definite object. When can I have a talk with you?'

'I shall be very glad. Will this evening do?'

'Yes. But one thing more. Don't speak about me, or say who I am. I have revealed myself only to you. No one knows where I have gone to. It must be so.'

'Oh, but I have told my daughter.'

'Well, ask her not to mention it.'

And Sergius took off his boots, lay down, and at once fell asleep after a sleepless night and a walk of nearly thirty miles.

When Praskovya Mikhaylovna returned, Sergius was sitting in the little room waiting for her. He did not come out for dinner, but had some soup and gruel which Lukerya brought him.

'How is it that you have come back earlier than you said?' asked Sergius. 'Can I speak to you now?'

'How is it that I have the happiness to receive such a guest? I have missed one of my lessons. That can wait . . . I had always been planning to go to see you. I wrote to you, and now this good fortune has come.'

'Pashenka, please listen to what I am going to tell you as to a confession made to God at my last hour. Pashenka, I am not a holy man, I am not even as good as a simple ordinary man; I am a loathsome, vile, and proud sinner who has gone astray, and who, if not worse than everyone else, is at least worse than most very bad people.'

Pashenka looked at him at first with staring eyes. But she believed what he said, and when she had quite grasped it she touched his hand, smiled pityingly, and said:

'Perhaps you exaggerate, Stiva?'

'No, Pashenka. I am an adulterer, a murderer, a blasphemer, and a deceiver.'

'My God! How is that?' exclaimed Praskovya Mikhaylovna.

'But I must go on living. And I, who thought I knew everything, who taught others how to live—I know nothing and ask you to teach me.'

'What are you saying, Stiva? You are laughing at me. Why do you always make fun of me?'

'Well, if you think I am jesting you must have it as you please. But tell me all the same how you live, and how you have lived your life.'

'I? I have lived a very nasty, horrible life, and now God is punishing me as I deserve. I live so wretchedly, so wretchedly...'

'How was it with your marriage? How did you live with your husband?'

'It was all bad. I married because I fell in love in the nastiest way. Papa did not approve. But I would not listen to anything and just got married. Then instead of helping my husband I tormented him by my jealousy, which I could not restrain.'

'I heard that he drank...'

'Yes, but I did not give him any peace. I always reproached him, though you know it's a disease! He could not refrain from it. I now remember how I tried to prevent his having it, and the frightful scenes we had!'

And she looked at Kasatsky with beautiful eyes, suffering from the remembrance.

Kasatsky remembered how he had been told that Pashenka's husband used to beat her, and now, looking at her thin withered neck with prominent veins behind her ears, and her scanty coil of hair, half grey half auburn, he seemed to see just how it had occurred.

'Then I was left with two children and no means at all.'

'But you had an estate!'

'Oh, we sold that while Vasya was still alive, and the money was all spent. We had to live, and like all our young ladies I did not know how to earn anything. I was particularly useless and helpless. So we spent all we had. I taught the children and improved my own education a little. And then Mitya fell ill when he was already in the fourth form, and God took him, Masha fell in love with Vanya, my son-in-law. And—well, he is well-meaning but unfortunate. He is ill.'

'Mamma!'—her daughter's voice interrupted her—'Take Mitya! I can't be in two places at once.'

Praskovya Mikhaylovna shuddered, but rose and went out of the room, stepping quickly in her patched shoes. She soon came back with a boy of two in her arms, who threw himself backwards and grabbed at her shawl with his little hands.

'Where was I? Oh yes, he had a good appointment here, and his chief was a kind man too. But Vanya could not go on, and had to give up his position.'

'What is the matter with him?'

'Neurasthenia—it is a dreadful complaint. We consulted a doctor, who told us he ought to go away, but we had no means. . . . I always hope it will pass of itself. He has no particular pain, but . . .'

'Lukerya!' cried an angry and feeble voice. 'She is always sent away when I want her. Mamma . . .'

'I'm coming!' Praskovya Mikhaylovna again interrupted herself. 'He has not had his dinner yet. He can't eat with us.'

She went out and arranged something, and came back wiping her thin dark hands.

'So that is how I live. I always complain and am always dissatisfied, but thank God the grandchildren are all nice and healthy, and we can still live. But why talk about me?'

'But what do you live on?'

'Well, I earn a little. How I used to dislike music, but how useful it is to me now!' Her small hand lay on the chest of drawers beside which she was sitting, and she drummed an exercise with her thin fingers.

'How much do you get for a lesson?'

'Sometimes a ruble, sometimes fifty kopeks, or sometimes thirty. They are all so kind to me.'

'And do your pupils get on well?' asked Kasatsky with a slight smile.

Praskovya Mikhaylovna did not at first believe that he was asking seriously, and looked inquiringly into his eyes.

'Some of them do. One of them is a splendid girl—the butcher's daughter—such a good kind girl! If I were a clever woman I ought, of course, with the connections Papa had, to be able to get an appointment for my son-in-law. But as it is I have not been able to do anything, and have brought them all to this—as you see.'

'Yes, yes,' said Kasatsky, lowering his head. 'And how is it, Pashenka—do you take part in church life?'

'Oh, don't speak of it. I am so bad that way, and have neglected it so! I keep the fasts with the children and sometimes go to church, and then again sometimes I don't go for months. I only send the children.'

'But why don't you go yourself?'

'To tell the truth' (she blushed) 'I am ashamed, for my daughter's sake and the children's to go there in tattered clothes, and I haven't anything else. Besides, I'm just lazy.'

'And do you pray at home?'

'I do. But what sort of prayer is it? Only mechanical. I know it should not be like that, but I lack real religious feeling. The only thing is that I know how bad I am . . .'

'Yes, yes, that's right!' said Kasatsky, as if approvingly.

'I'm coming! I'm coming!' she replied to a call from her son-in-law, and straightening her scanty plait she left the room.

But this time it was long before she returned. When she came back, Kasatsky was sitting in the same position, his elbows resting on his knees and his head bowed. But his scrip was strapped on his back.

When she came in, carrying a small tin lamp without a shade, he raised his fine weary eyes and sighed very deeply.

'I did not tell them who you are,' she began timidly. 'I only said that you are a pilgrim, a nobleman, and that I used to know you. Come into the dining-room for tea.'

'No . . .'

'Well then, I'll bring some to you here.'

'No, I don't want anything. God bless you, Pahenka! I am going now. If you pity me, don't tell anyone that you have seen me. For the love of God don't tell anyone. Thank you. I would bow to your feet but I know it would make you feel awkward. Thank you, and forgive me for Christ's sake!'

'Give me your blessing.'

'God bless you! Forgive me for Christ's sake!'

He rose, but she would let him go until she had given him bread and butter and rusks. He took it all and went away.

It was dark, and before he had passed the second house he was lost to sight. She only knew he was there because the dog at the priest's house was barking.

'So that is what my dream meant! Pashenka is what I ought to have been but failed to be. I lived for men on the pretext of living for God, while she lives for God imagining that she lives for men. Yes, one good deed—a cup of water given without thought of reward—is worth more than any benefit I imagined I was bestowing on people. But after all was there not some share of sincere desire to serve God?' he asked himself, and the answer was: 'Yes, there was, but it was all soiled and overgrown by desire for human praise. Yes, there is no God for the man who lives, as I did, for human praise. I will now seek Him!'

And he walked from village to village as he had done on his way to Pashenka, meeting and parting from other pilgrims, men and women, and asking for bread and a night's rest in Christ's name. Occasionally some angry housewife scolded him, or a drunken peasant reviled him, but for the most part he was given food and drink and even something to take with him. His noble bearing disposed some people in his favour, while others on the contrary seemed pleased at the sight of a gentleman who had come to beggary.

But his gentleness prevailed with everyone.

Often, finding a copy of the Gospels in a hut he would read it aloud, and when they heard him the people were always touched and surprised, as at something new yet familiar.

When he succeeded in helping people, either by advice, or by his knowledge of reading and writing, or by settling some quarrel, he did not wait to see their gratitude but went away directly afterwards. And little by little God began to reveal Himself within him.

Once he was walking along with two old women and a soldier. They were stopped by a party consisting of a lady and gentleman in a gig and another lady and gentleman on horseback. The husband was on horseback with his daughter, while in the gig his wife was driving with a Frenchman, evidently a traveller.

The party stopped to let the Frenchman see the pilgrims who, in accord with a popular Russian superstition, tramped about from place to place instead of working.

They spoke French, thinking that the others would not understand them.

'*Demandez-leur,*' said the Frenchman, '*s'ils sont bien sûr de ce que leur pèlerinage est agréable à Dieu.*'

The question was asked, and one old woman replied: 'As God takes it. Our feet have reached the holy places, but our hearts may not have done so.'

They asked the soldier. He said that he was alone in the world and had nowhere else to go.

They asked Kasatsky who he was.

'A servant of God.'

'*Qu'est-ce qu'il dit? Il ne répond pas.*'

'*Il dit qu'il est un serviteur de Dieu. Cela doit être un fils de prêtre. Il a de la race. Avez-vous de la petite monnaie?*'

The Frenchman found some small change and gave twenty kopeks to each of the pilgrims.

'*Mais dites-leur que ce n'est pas pour les cierges que je leur donne, mais pour qu'ils se régalent de thé. Chay, chay pour vous, mon vieux!*' he said with a smile. And he patted Kasatsky on the shoulder with his gloved hand.

'May Christ bless you,' replied Kasatsky without replacing his cap and bowing his bald head.

He rejoiced particularly at this meeting, because he had disregarded the opinion of men and had done the simplest, easiest thing—humbly accepted twenty kopeks and given them to his comrade, a blind beggar. The less importance he attached to the opinion of men the more did he feel the presence of God within him.

For eight months Kasatsky tramped on in this manner, and in the ninth month he was arrested for not having a passport. This happened at a night-refuge in a provincial town where he had passed the night with some pilgrims. He was taken to the police-station, and when asked who he was and where was his passport, he replied that he had no passport and that he was a servant of God. He was classed as a tramp, sentenced, and sent to live in Siberia.

In Siberia he had settled down as the hired man of a well-to-do peasant, in which capacity he works in the kitchen-garden, teaches children, and attends to the sick.

also available from
CAPUCHIN CLASSICS

How I Became a Holy Mother and other stories
Ruth Prawer Jhabvala. Introduced by Francis King
'Every one of them is brilliant. They are richly, slyly comic and quite desperately sad… that sharp eye for the give-away gesture, that keen perception of human loneliness and the various guises it assumes. In her quiet, undemonstrative way, Ruth Prawer Jhabvala is a truly astonishing writer.' *Observer*

Plain Tales from the Hills
Rudyard Kipling. Introduced by Griff Rhys Jones
'These stories are the best account of the nature of the Victorian Raj ever written.' Griff Rhys Jones

The Incredulity of Father Brown
GK Chesterton. Introduced by Ann Widdecombe
Sensation followed the sudden death of Chesterton's eccentric sleuth; as well it might, when he sat up in his coffin and applied a little quiet detachment to the incident. But then sensation was implicit in all the cases Father Brown so modestly handled.

Love in a Wych Elm
HE Bates. Introduced by Peter Conradi
Kent, the 'Garden of England', provides the rustic setting for these poignant stories from the creator of *The Darling Buds of May*. Graham Greene liked to compare HE Bates with Chekhov, greatest of short story writers, considering Bates the best writer of short stories of his generation and time. This new selection by Bates' grandson, Tim Bates, shows why.

www.capuchin-classics.co.uk